PRAISE FOR WHITE HOUSES

"Bloom's lyrical novel, laced with her characteristic wit and wisdom, celebrates love in its fiery and also embered phases. . . . Bloom's gift to Lorena Hickok is to shine not just light but also laughter on this neglected figure, highlighting the two women's shared humor, including acknowledgment of their famously unfeminine appearance. . . . In Bloom's eloquent telling, the love these two women had for each other mattered, and lasted, in a significant way.

—*The New York Times Book Review*

"Breathtakingly intimate and with the grandest of historical sweeps . . . What Bloom gives us is the grace and dignity of clear-eyed, enduring, imperfect love. . . . If *White Houses* isn't an example of the great American novel then frankly, I don't know what is."

—*Financial Times*

"If you like to make a meal out of ungarnished facts, stick to the history books. But *White Houses* serves up a plate piled with delectable trimmings. . . . With its adoring portrait of Eleanor Roosevelt, *White Houses* reminds us what true greatness looks like. It also demonstrates that the god of love has yet again found a welcoming hangout in Bloom's bighearted fiction."

—*San Francisco Chronicle*

"Fictionalized accounts of the lives of real people in history have been all the rage lately, but few are as pitch perfect and fascinating as Amy Bloom's take on Lorena Hickok, the woman who Eleanor Roosevelt loved. Hick's relationship with the president's wife comes vividly and tenderly to life, even as the two women must contain their love to hidden corners of the White House."

—*Esquire*

"Bloom deftly explores what might have been in this novel about the real romance between Eleanor Roosevelt and journalist Lorena Hickok. . . . It's a sensuous, captivating account of a forbidden affair between two women, one of them viewed by all the world as a saint."

—*People*

"'All fires go out,' Hickok says, explaining her lingering feelings to Franklin. 'It doesn't mean that we don't still want to sit by the fireplace, I guess.' In *White Houses,* Bloom has built up exactly the sort of blaze that will draw readers to linger."

—*Time*

"Exquisite . . . A book about politics both personal and global, a love story that captures an era, *White Houses* is nothing short of extraordinary."

—*The Sydney Morning Herald*

"Vivid and tender . . . Bloom—interweaving fact and fancy—lavishes attention on [Lorena Hickok], bringing Hick, the novel's narrator and true subject, to radiant life."

—*O: The Oprah Magazine*

"[An] irresistibly audacious re-creation of the love affair between Eleanor Roosevelt and journalist Lorena "Hick" Hickok . . . Bloom convincingly weaves tender romance with hard-boiled reality. . . . Bloom notes that the White House staff routinely cropped Hickok out of photos. In *White Houses,* she's in the center of the frame, and nobody who reads this sad, funny, frisky novel is going to forget her."

—*USA Today*

"Radiant . . . an indelible love story, one propelled not by unlined youth and beauty but by the kind of soul-mate connection even distance, age, and impossible circumstances couldn't dim . . . [Bloom's] goal is less to relitigate history than to portray the blandly sexless figurehead of First Lady as something the job rarely allows those women to be—a loving, breathing human being. And she does it brilliantly."

—*Entertainment Weekly*

"Steeped with open secrets, intimate tension, and historical truths, [*White Houses*] expertly portrays the kaleidoscopic forms womanhood can take."

—*New York*

"Profoundly affecting . . . Bloom's Hick is frank, funny, and irreverent. . . . *White Houses*, by seeing the Roosevelt era through the most unlikely of outsiders-turned-insider, brings a hidden chapter of East Wing history to life."

—*The Boston Globe*

"From the beloved author of *Lucky Us* and *Away* comes a historical fiction about the forbidden love affair between Eleanor Roosevelt and Lorena Hickok. Need I say more? You're obviously going to be hooked."

—*Bustle*

"In *White Houses*, Amy Bloom illuminates this relationship and Hickok's tumultuous life with her usual evocative prose, making readers reflect on what they would do for true love."

—*Real Simple*

"Amy Bloom always captures love on the page honestly and lushly. . . . [*White Houses*] is a towering love story of two remarkable women."

—*St. Louis Post-Dispatch*

"Smart and tender . . . Bloom chronicles this complex affair, and in Hick, who narrates the book, she creates an engaging, poignant, self-aware character who's a delight to spend time with."

—*Tampa Bay Times*

"As this captivating book's narrator, [Hick's voice is] considerately blunt, compassionately unsparing, reliably truth-telling and strong-pulsed. And it's the master of its own cadence, clipped and to the point in its journalistic guise, then vaulting at the sheer thrill of storytelling. . . . Bloom also has a gift for telling her/their story out of chronological order without once confusing or losing her reader. Some of her most masterful transitions are as invisible as the seams of the dresses she describes with the acuity of Alexander Chee."

—*The Bay Area Reporter*

"Bloom has always worked best up close, near her characters' heads and hearts and sheets, and *White Houses* brings the reader inside a love affair for the ages."

—*The Dallas Morning News*

"A heartbreaking, beautiful novel . . . Bloom brings the Roosevelts and their world vividly to life and gives an unforgettable voice to the larger-than-life Lorena. . . . An original, richly textured, and beautifully written love story."

—*Library Journal*

"Bloom uncloaks the insidious treacheries girls and women face, poor and privileged alike. . . . [A] socially incisive, psychologically saturated, funny, and erotic fictionalization of legendary figures . . . [a] novel of extraordinary magnetism and insight; [a] keen celebration of love, loyalty, and sacrifice."

—*Booklist* (starred review)

"An achingly beautiful love story . . . Bloom brings incredible dimension to her historical figures, especially the wise and savvy Hick. . . . *White Houses* is so gorgeously written that some passages need to be read more than once, or perhaps aloud, to fully appreciate their craftsmanship. A Roosevelt cousin describes Hick as erudite. To call this novel the same would be an understatement."

—*BookPage*

"Bloom elevates this addition to the secret-lives-of-the-Roosevelts genre through elegant prose and by making Lorena Hickok a character engrossing enough to steal center stage from Eleanor Roosevelt. . . . Lorena's winning narrative voice is tough, gossipy, and deeply humane."

—*Kirkus Reviews* (starred review)

"Cleverly structured through reminiscences that slowly build in intimacy, Bloom's passionate novel beautifully renders the hidden love of one of America's most guarded first ladies."

—*Publishers Weekly*

"A remarkably intimate and yet informative novel of the secret, scandalous love of Eleanor Roosevelt and her longtime friend and companion Lorena Hickok, who relates the tale in her own, quite wonderful voice."

—JOYCE CAROL OATES

"Amy Bloom illuminates one of the most intriguing relationships in history. Lorena Hickok is a woman who found love with another lost soul, Eleanor Roosevelt. And love is what this book is all about: It suffuses every page, so that by the time you reach the end, you are simply stunned by the beauty of the world these two carved out for themselves."

—MELANIE BENJAMIN, author of *The Swans of Fifth Avenue*

"It seems a minor miracle, what Amy Bloom has done in *White Houses*. In Lorena Hickok's unforgettable voice, she brings an untold slice of history so dazzlingly and devastatingly to life, it took my breath away. This is easily the most intimate, crackling, and expansive rendering of Eleanor Roosevelt in print and, more than that, a dizzyingly beautiful tale of what it means to be human, and what it is to love."

—PAULA McLAIN, author of *The Paris Wife*

BY AMY BLOOM

WHITE HOUSES

RANDOM HOUSE
New York

Amy Bloom

WHITE HOUSES

A Novel

2018 Random House Trade Paperback Edition

Published in the United States by Random House, an imprint and division of Penguin Random House LLC, New York.

RANDOM HOUSE and the HOUSE colophon are registered trademarks of Penguin Random House LLC.

RANDOM HOUSE READER'S CIRCLE & Design is a registered trademark of Penguin Random House LLC.

Originally published in hardcover in the United States by Random House, an imprint and division of Penguin Random House LLC, in 2018.

Grateful acknowledgment is made to the following for permission to reprint preexisting material:

Daily News: Excerpt from "The Day Charles Lindbergh's Baby Was Kidnapped in 1932" (3/2/32), © Daily News, L.P. (New York). Used with permission.

Nancy Roosevelt Ireland, Executor, Eleanor Roosevelt Estate: Telegram to Lorena Hickock, November 8, 1962. Reprinted by permission of Nancy Roosevelt Ireland, Executor, Eleanor Roosevelt Estate.

LIBRARY OF CONGRESS CATALOGING-IN-PUBLICATION DATA
Names: Bloom, Amy, author.
Title: White houses: a novel / Amy Bloom.
Description: New York: Random House, [2018]
Identifiers: LCCN 2017028296 | ISBN 9780812985696 | ISBN 9780812995671 (ebook)
Subjects: LCSH: Roosevelt, Eleanor, 1884–1962—Fiction. | Hickock, Lorena A.—Fiction. | Presidents' spouses—Fiction. | Women journalists—Fiction. |
GSAFD: Biographical fiction. | Historical fiction.
Classification: LCC ps3552.L6378 w48 2018 | DDC 813/.54—dc23
LC record available at https://lccn.loc.gov/2017028296

Printed in the United States of America on acid-free paper

randomhousebooks.com
randomhousereaderscircle.com

9 8 7 6 5 4 3 2 1

Book design by Simon M. Sullivan

For my parents, Sydelle and Murray

Contents

PART FOUR

WHITE HOUSES

Prologue

....

FRIDAY AFTERNOON, APRIL 27, 1945
29 Washington Square West
New York, New York

No love like old love.

I've done the flowers as best I could. I got stock and snap-dragons, pink roses and daffodils, from the Italian florist and I've put a vaseful in every room. I've straightened up the four rooms, which were already neat. The radio still works. The record player works too, and someone has brought in albums of Cole Porter and Gershwin and there is one scratchy record of *La Bohème* with Lisa Perli from when I was a more regular visitor. I've gone to the corner grocery twice (eggs, milk, bread, horseradish cheese, sardines, and I went back again because there was no can opener) and up the street one more time, for booze. I hope that at five o'clock, we'll be drinking sidecars. I bought lemons. I want to have everything we need close by. I am hoping we don't see so much as the lobby all weekend.

I change my clothes in the living room. I don't think I should be in the bedroom, at all, unless I get invited. I anticipate sleeping on the couch. I've brought my navy-blue Sulka pajamas, for old times' sake.

On the radio, the newsman raises his voice like a coach on the field, and says that the eighteen major cities of Germany are *ablaze*. He says, the Potsdam Division of the German army is systematically murdering the Americans wounded on the battle-field. He says, with a lilt, that two thousand American planes are attacking rail positions near Berlin and other communications centers in southern Germany. He says, Good night, ladies and gentlemen, victory is in sight. I hope so.

I'm glad and I'm tired. I'll celebrate the war's end out on Long Island, with a couple of other old broads and our dogs, and we will all toast Franklin Roosevelt, who didn't live to see it. My neighbor Gloria and I will sing "Straighten Up and Fly Right." Every single one of us will cry.

I sit down on the living room couch to wait. I used to be able to read Eleanor's heart, when I saw her face, and I worry that I can't anymore. I expect to see her gray with Roosevelt suffering, the kind that must not only be borne but must be seen to be borne, elegantly, showing her great effort to be patient with everyone's sadness and pulling need and beneath that, just like it was with her brother, a hook of barbed and furious grief that she'd tear out if she could. She told me that nothing on earth was worse than losing her baby, the first Franklin Junior, but I sat with her for the long days of her brother Hall's death, and she cried for him, every night, as if he hadn't broken everybody's hearts, as if he hadn't almost killed one of his own children and ruined the other five. She sat by Hall's bed, looking like that Henry Adams statue she used to drag me to, the monument of transcendent misery Adams put up when his wife killed herself with cyanide. That's what I am expecting, but I hope that in the mix of her feelings for Franklin, sorrow at his death, and grief for her children and for the country, she'll be glad to see me. I want her to feel that with me, she's home, like it used to be. She sent me away eight years ago, and I left. Two days ago, she called me to come and I came.

The buzzer rings, which means her hands are full and she can't get to her key.

I open the door and Eleanor is leaning against the wall, paper white.

Her beautiful blue eyes are red-rimmed, all the way around, and she looks as if she has never smiled in her life. Her dusty black coat is enormous on her, and her lisle stockings bag. I kiss her because I always kiss her hello, when we are alone and we're on speaking terms, and she turns her cheek toward me and looks away. She hands me her purse and her suitcase. I put down the bags and I put my arm around her waist. I try to pull her face to mine but she turns away and rests one hand on my shoulder, to take off her shoes.

She drops her hat, coat, and scarf on the big brocade armchair. She unbuttons her gray blouse and lets it fall to the floor. She walks into the bedroom, unzips her skirt, and I follow behind, picking up as we go. She sits on the edge of the bed in a ragged white slip she should have thrown out long before the war.

She takes the pins out of her gray hair and pulls off her awful lisle stockings. We fought about those stockings. I said that even in a war, the First Lady did not actually have to entertain royalty while wearing knit cotton stockings and she said that was exactly what the First Lady had to do. I stretch the stockings over the arm of the club chair and she shrugs.

She lies down on the bed, facing the wall, and lifts her right arm up behind her. Without turning to face me, she beckons me over.

"Well, Queen of England," I say.

She drops her arm. This is not my Eleanor. I used to weep

when she was stern and gracious with me, explaining my faults until I curled up like a snail on a bed of salt. She'd sit still and tragically disappointed for an hour or more, until I begged forgiveness. That's my sweetheart. This waxy indifference is new.

I pile her clothes on the wood chair. I put her black shoes in front of the fireplace. I hang her black coat in the closet, next to my navy-blue one, and my red scarf falls over them both. I'm sorry I've come.

Oh, Hick, she says, if you don't hold me, I will die.

I climb in behind her and she undresses me with one long white hand, still not turning. I look out over her shoulder and watch people turn on their lights.

Eleven years ago we had our golden time and our first vacation. Maine and beyond was our golden hour. Hoover was out. Franklin was in. We all moved into the White House, friends, family, and me.

Eleanor and I had had our first private lunch at the White House, grinning and posing in front of the portraits like teenage girls. Why don't you move in, she said. We have so much room.

I asked her what she meant and she said, again, We have so much room. I leaned over to kiss her and she pushed me away a little. I have some housekeeping to do, if you're coming, she said. Why don't you go and get your things?

I went back to Brooklyn and put my rent check, almost the full amount, in the mail. I drove my blue suitcase, my Underwood Portable, and a box of books down to D.C. the next day. One of the housekeepers took me through the White House, up the stairs to Eleanor's suite, blank and polite, as if she'd never seen me before, as if she'd never done my laundry or hemmed my skirt when

I'd stayed for the weekend, but when she opened the door to my room, she smiled and put my typewriter on the desk. My new room adjoined Eleanor's; it was her old sitting room.

I had a big desk, a bookshelf, and an old Windsor chair. I had two table lamps and a floor lamp. I had a bed, a dark velvet couch that had seen better days, which I pushed toward the corner, and an oak armoire big enough to hide in. The only thing between us was a wall covered with photographs and an old wooden door.

I spent about an hour, sitting upright on my twin bed, my hat and coat still on, staring at that door, willing it to let me in, to look down on the Rose Garden, to let me open the window to the big magnolia tree.

Eleanor finally came in and sat down next to me.

"I shower people with love, because I like to," she said. "I like showering people with love. You've seen me, with my friends."

I had. It already drove me crazy.

She said, "I want you to know, besides my friends, I have had crushes. I'll find someone, often someone wonderful, but really, they don't have to be, and I adore them, no matter what. Doctor Freud would say it's my mother all over again. Or my father."

She took off my hat, laughing. I did not do or say a single charming, clever thing. I rubbed my knuckles.

"I am determined to tell you what I want to tell you," she said. "About the crushes. Because people may tell you, that I'm prone. That this is a crush. Someone looks into my eyes, and they see a whole world of love that I have for them. And they love that, and they love me, for the way I love them. They look into my eyes and see themselves at the very center of the world. And people do love that."

She walked over to the wooden door and twisted the knob a few times.

"This thing always sticks."

"Come back," I said.

She sat back down on the bed, and held my hand, looking straight ahead.

"You see me. You see all of me and I don't think you love everything you see. I hope you do, but I doubt you do. But, you see me. The whole person. Not just yourself, reflected in my eyes. Not just the person who loves you. Me."

My ears burned, the way they did after three Scotches.

Now, she turned and faced me.

"Lorena Alice Hickock, you are the surprise of my life. I love you. I love your nerve. I love your laugh. I love your way with a sentence. I love your beautiful eyes and your beautiful skin and I will love you till the day I die."

I pushed out the words before she could change her mind.

"Anna Eleanor Roosevelt, you amazing, perfect, imperfect woman, you have knocked me sideways. I love you. I love your kindness and your brilliance and your soft heart. I love how you dance and I love your beautiful hands and I will love you till the day I die."

I took off my sapphire ring and slipped it onto her pinkie. She unpinned the gold watch from her lapel and pinned it on my shirt. She put her arms around my waist. We kissed as if we were in the midst of a cheering crowd, with rice and rose petals raining down on us.

All the way to the Associated Press office, I kept my hand on the gold watch. I knew I had to resign. I'd already quashed a dozen prizewinning Roosevelt stories to protect her, or him, or the kids. I needed to change my beat or give her up.

I did resign. Also, I was fired. I offered to cover some other beat, Wall Street or city crime. My editor pushed back in his chair, folded his hands over his great belly, and looked at me like I was the worst kind of cockroach. You're part of the story, kid, he said. He said, I got the greatest inside track to the White House, ever, and I'm not giving that up. In that case, I said, I have to resign altogether. He shrugged like he'd never expected anything more and we shook hands.

Some old pals watched me empty my desk and no one offered to buy me a drink. The woman who did weddings waved, cheerfully. The sportswriter shook his head. The obit guy lifted his hat. (What do you call the Jewish gentleman who leaves the room? Bernard Baruch said to me. A kike.) I had twenty-five dollars in my bank account and no job prospects.

All the way back to the White House, I reminded myself that I was good, that I was honorable, that there was depth and beauty to my sacrifice and that integrity mattered. I wanted it to matter to Eleanor, who'd never had to get or quit a job, and she was delighted with me. She believed that all life worth living involved sacrifice and the more the better. This way, she said, we'll have more time together. This way, we will have our life. She meant that I wouldn't have to worry about betraying her and she wouldn't have to worry about my betraying her and I wouldn't spend so much time with rumpled men who swore and drank Scotch before noon. She hugged me and said, I think this is for the best, Dearest. Franklin rolled by, on cue and said, We got a job for you, Hicky.

I never found out which one of them thought of it first, but they both told me to go talk to Harry Hopkins, who was looking for an investigative reporter to help him run Federal Emergency Relief. (You report back to Harry, about how bad it is out there, Franklin said. And just be a reporter, not a social worker.) They both told me the pay would be better than what I got at the Associated Press. Hopkins hired me in ten minutes, holding my résumé behind his back and looking out a window as if he were reading from a script. Thank you, Miss Hickock, I'll rely on your reports, he said, still looking away.

I ran back to tell Eleanor that I got the job and she smiled.

At five o'clock, another maid came and told me to go downstairs for drinks. Franklin and Eleanor toasted me. Franklin said, Much better to have you inside the tent, Hick, and pissing out.

We planned a vacation. (I want to see everything with you, Eleanor said.) We talked Franklin out of sending the Secret Service with us and we loaded up the car and waved to him from the driveway. He waved from the front porch. Behave yourselves, he shouted. We waved one more time.

We thought we knew everything about each other that mattered and none of what would come to matter was even a mote in our golden light. We had new love and this beautiful country, reckless and wide. We had Eleanor's very sporty light-blue Buick roadster and enough money for everything we wanted, or even were just in the mood for. Eleanor wrapped her hair in a scarf and dangled one arm over the side of the car, like a movie star. We glided from place to place, in love, in rapture, enjoying each day, all day, and moving on, just so as to enjoy more.

We camped and talked. I sang to Eleanor, every hymn I'd ever learned and dirty songs to make her put her hands over her ears. (A lot of things rhyme with Hick.) We loaded the backseat with bags of pretzels, brand-new sunglasses, a stack of maps, a bag of Eleanor's knitting, which made me laugh, a deck of cards, just in case, and books of poetry. (*Wild nights,* I recited, while she drove. *Wild nights, were I but moored in thee.* Moored, I yelled again, until she blushed. I admire Emily Dickinson, Eleanor said.)

I'd packed my navy pajamas and she'd packed her pink nightgown and one night, in a nearly empty hotel in Vermont, she put on the pajamas and I put on the nightgown and we almost broke the bed. She wrote to Franklin regularly. Just so that he won't worry, she said. Send my regards, I said. Sometimes people recognized her, and we'd stop and I'd back away, to the car, or into a shop, so she could sip the lemonade or the cider, and admire the children or the goats or the quilts, and pose for a picture if someone had a camera, which they rarely did, because we were so far from the modern world, up there. She'd started out as not much of a public speaker and she'd made herself a good one. She couldn't tell a joke to save her life. But Eleanor could listen. Every person she spoke to was her hero. Angry logger, blind widow with a Rose of Sharon quilt, hopeful musician, grateful nurse at the end of the graveyard shift, mother of six with her hand crushed in the factory. She came close. She bent her head toward yours and she slowed and she listened. She settled and got still. She didn't look, for a second, as if she was thinking about anything except your story. If you hesitated because you were worn-out or embarrassed, she leaned forward as if she couldn't bear that you would now, in the middle of this moment between you, turn away from her.

We love the attentiveness of powerful people, because it's such a pleasant, gratifying surprise, but Eleanor was not a grand light shining briefly on the lucky little people. She reached for the soul of everyone who spoke to her, every day. She bowed her head toward yours, as if there was nothing but the time and necessary space for two people to briefly love each other.

Mostly we met farmers and elderly Republicans, people who

didn't look at newspapers, if they could help it, except for local news and sports and feed prices. Mostly, we were, as we liked to pretend, Jane and Janet Doe, walking arm in arm, talking mouth to ear. Middle-aged women who liked each other: sisters, cousins, best friends. We kept ourselves to ourselves, except for Eleanor's strong wish to be pleasant to everyone, and mostly people thought of us whatever people think of middle-aged ladies and that's all.

We took a break from the goats and quilts and Eleanor drove us to Quebec, to Château Frontenac, telling me, as we got to the outskirts, Close your eyes. I think when I am an old lady, when people have to shout to get my attention, you could murmur, Château Frontenac, and I will smile like a cat paw-deep in cream. Eleanor did for us what she never liked doing for herself and she did it on a grand scale, with gilt edges. We sat, I should say, we cavorted, in the French Canadian lap of luxury. We got massages together with two strong ladies coming into our suite with two massage tables, picnic baskets of warm towels, and rose and orange oils. I pretended that I'd somehow wandered in from the hideaway bed in the living room. They set up the tables and indicated we should strip and wrap ourselves in sheets. We did and we tottered over to the tables, to be rubbed and patted by these two frowning women who couldn't understand our language. Our faces were only two feet apart, our bodies glistening with rose-scented oil.

I said, "This is too much."

"I know," Eleanor said. "We have manicures after lunch."

I said to Eleanor, This is our trip to Erewhon and she agreed. Our particular Nowhere, she said, will be found at the northern tip of Maine. Grab your sweater. We drove to a cabin overlooking the ocean at dusk and unpacked before dark. We shared a brandy and the last of the pretzels and stood in our nightclothes on the little porch, the big quilt around us. The mottled, bright white moon pulled the tide like a silver rug, onto the dark pebbled beach. It should have been a starry sky, but it was deep indigo, like the sea below, with nothing in it but the one North Star.

"I'm making a wish," I said.

We ate potato pancakes for breakfast. (Every café and diner featured potatoes. We had buttery and cheesy grated potatoes mounded in potato skins, which were delicious, and chocolate cake, enhanced with mashed potatoes, which was not.) We took walks and designed our dream cottage. Sometimes it was another version of her beloved Hyde Park cottage, Val-Kill, a rabbit warren of rooms with plenty of space, a library, and a communal dining room. Sometimes, it was a cottage on Long Island, where I now live, rose-covered and overlooking the Sound. One night, I made shadow puppets of everything we would see from our dream porch. I did a fox, a heron, a squirrel, and two people kissing, which is all the shadow puppetry I knew. We had tuna fish sandwiches on the rough, windy beach and furnished our dream apartment in Greenwich Village. We imagined trips to places neither of us had been. How about Gaspé Bay, I said. We've never been here before. Baie de Gaspé, she said. All right, I said. Let's add Upper Gaspé, Land's End, Chaleur Bay. Don't forget Armonk and Massapequa. All the nightspots.

I imagined Eleanor telling her children about us. If they'd been actual children, I would have liked my chances better. I'd have told them myself, if they were actual children. Children liked me. I was quick with the cookies, and slow to scold. I could bait a hook, build a house of cards, and make strawberry shortcake. I winked behind their mothers' backs when they had their hands on the last biscuit and I liked the feel of a small child on my shoulder. I was a natural but the Roosevelt boys were spoiled and empty and endlessly wanting and Anna was pretty and shrewd. She could've been a cooch dancer at L'Étoile du Nord, if she'd had a stronger work ethic. I felt for them all what the hardworking poor feel for the rich (not, by and large, admiration and affection) and they felt for me what children feel about that person who seems to have your mother's heart. I might be able to get Anna on my side but the thought of telling Eleanor's sons anything shut me up.

Eleanor pointed out that we did not have to make an announcement.

"It's not as if we're calling them into the Oval Office. There's no need for fuss," she said.

She sat the way she did when she lectured her children, spine straight, hands clasped. I threw a pillow at her and she ducked.

"It's the end of his term—"

"He'll have two terms," I said.

She frowned.

"Pretend I never spoke," I said. "Carry on."

"We say, 'My dears, now that Father is no longer president, he and I have the opportunity to continue in public service, and continue our marriage. But we will also go our separate ways.'"

"Which is nothing new," I said.

"That's correct. I say that Franklin and I will always be a team, of course."

"Of course," I said. "Boola boola."

"That's Yale," she said, shaking her head.

"And then Junior collapses likes he's been shot, Jimmy gets drunk, John asks for an increase in his allowance, and Elliott starts screaming about 'Who will look after poor Pater?'"

"Jimmy is not that big a drinker. I say to them, 'Your father and I love each other and our marriage will continue.' I say, 'You may visit him at Campobello and you may visit us . . .'"

She wiped her eyes.

"This is a silly game," she said. "When the time comes, you and I will move into Val-Kill, that's all."

"That's plenty," I said.

We think we'll remember it all and we remember hardly anything. Even when the car is only doing forty, it's still going too fast. The trees are a green and gray blur, the restaurant where we thought we'd die laughing over the misspelled menu has come and gone. Neon-green streaks and bolts of flamingo pink blow up the sky on a winter night in Maine and we think—oh, we will never forget these northern lights, but we do. What we remember is only the curling picture in the left-hand drawer (Presque Isle, Maine, 1934) or a gorgeous half-page photo in an old travel magazine, but what we saw when we held hands, lifting our chins to the sky as if we could leap into the jagged, jeweled brilliance above us, was seen for ten seconds only, and never again.

She loved the theater. She was mad for Cole Porter and there wasn't a song of his she didn't know. She nodded to everyone. She clasped every hand. The house lights dimmed and Eleanor kissed me, on the palm, and she whispered, in tune, *You're the top. You're Mahatma Gandhi. You're the top. You're Napoleon brandy.* I thought, I will remember this. And I do.

We were in the Rose Garden and ducked behind a tower of pale pink roses to kiss. We walked upstairs and past the Secret Service man and Eleanor said, Good evening, Wyatt. I'm in need of repair, and he said, very warmly, Yes, ma'am. She said, This party will run another two hours, don't you think, and he looked at his watch. That's what we were told, ma'am. We racewalked into her bedroom, as if we were hell-bent on finding safety pins. Her sequined jacket slid to the floor and with it her three-story white orchid corsage, which would have to reappear in an hour or so. She said, Do not touch that thing. She pulled me onto the bed. I didn't think, I have to remember this. But I have.

PART ONE

Luck Is Not Chance

. . . .

In 1932, my father was dead and my star was rising. I could write. People looked for my name. I'd gotten a big bounce from *The Milwaukee Sentinel* to New York because I was the only woman to cover Big Ten football playoffs *and* the excellent Smith scandal (idiot corset salesman and buxom mistress cut off the head of her husband and hide it in the bathtub). I had hit it hard in Brooklyn, at the *Daily Mirror* and moved on to the Associated Press. I had a small apartment, with a palm-sized window and a bathroom down the hall. I owned one frying pan, two plates, and two coffee mugs. My friends were newspapermen, my girlfriends were often copy editors (very sharp, very sweet), and I was what they called a newspaperwoman. They ran my bylines and everyone knew I didn't do weddings. It was good.

The men bought me drinks and every night I bought a round before I went home. They talked about their wives and mistresses in front of me and I didn't blink. I didn't wrinkle my nose. I sympathized. When the wives were on the rag, when the girlfriend had a bun in the oven, when the door was locked, I said it was a damn shame. I sipped my Scotch. I kept my chin up and my eyes friendly. I didn't tell the guys that I was no different, that I'd sooner bed a dozen wrong girls and wake up in a dozen hot-sheet joints, minus my wallet and plus a few scratches, than be tied down to one woman and a couple of brats. I pretended that even though I hadn't found the right man, I did want one. I pretended that I envied their wives and that took effort.

(I never envied a wife or a husband, until I met Eleanor. Then, I would have traded everything I ever had, every limo ride, every skinny-dip, every byline and carefree stroll, for what Franklin had, polio and all.)

It was a perfect night to be in a Brooklyn bar, waiting for the snow to fall. I signaled for another beer and a young man, from the city desk, stout and red-faced like me, brought it over and said, "Hick, is your dad Addison Hickok? I remember you were from South Dakota."

I said, Yes, that was me, and that was my old man.

I'm sorry, he said, I hear he killed himself. It came over the wire, there was a rash of Dust Bowl suicides. Traveling salesman, right? I'm sorry.

Don't you worry, I said. I couldn't say, Drinks all around, because my father's dead and I am not just glad, I am goddamn glad. No man drinks to a woman saying that. I left two bits under my glass and made my way home, to find a letter from Miz Min, my father's second wife, asking if I might send money for the burial expenses. I lit the envelope with my cigarette and I went to New Jersey.

I was the Associated Press's top dog for the Lindbergh kidnapping. We were all racing to tell the story and the *Daily News* got there first, with an enormous, grainy photo of the baby and the headline "Lindy's Baby Kidnaped," which was clear and short, and the *Times*'s "Lindbergh Baby Kidnapped from Home of Parents on Farm Near Princeton" was more exact but not first. They avoided vulgar familiarity but really, who cares whether the baby's taken from a farm or a ranch or a clover patch.

(THE DAILY NEWS, MARCH 2, 1932.)

The most famous baby in the world, Charles A. Lindbergh Jr., was kidnaped from his crib on the first floor of the Lone Eagle's home at Hopewell, N.J., between 7:30 and 10:30 o'clock last night.

The flier's wife, the former Anne Morrow, discovered at 10:30 that her 20-months-old son was missing. Her mother, Mrs. Dwight W. Morrow, who disclosed that Mrs. Lindbergh is expecting another baby, feared that the shock might have serious effect.

Anne immediately called Col. Lindbergh, who was in the living room. The famous flier, thinking that the nurse might have removed the child, paused to investigate before telephoning the State police.

As rapidly as radio, telephone and telegraph could spread the alarm countrywide, the biggest police hunt in history was under way.

Seventy State Troopers from Morristown, Trenton, Somerville and Lambertsville hopped on motorcycles and in automobiles and began to race over the countryside for a radius of a hundred miles around Princeton, which is ten miles west of the Lindbergh residence.

At midnight the teletype alarm had been spread over five States. Commissioner Edward P. Mulrooney, aroused from sleep, personally took control of the New York City search, which included scrutiny of all ferries, tunnels and bridges. Police in Pennsylvania, Delaware and Connecticut were also spreading a gigantic net.

CHILD CARRIED THROUGH WINDOW

The Lindbergh baby had been dressed in his sleeping gown by his nurse, and was asleep in the nursery on the first floor of the country mansion when he was kidnaped. The child was taken out of a window, through which the kidnaper or gang of kidnapers apparently entered the home.

A note, contents not disclosed, was found on the second floor of the home. Whether this was a demand for ransom could not be learned - although that was the assumption in some quarters.

This went on for a few more columns, bringing in the neighbor with the green car (who had nothing to do with anything) and recounting the loving, playful disagreement the Lindberghs apparently had over what to name the baby in the first place, using sentiment (What shall we name the Little Eaglet?) to underscore the strong and irresistible likelihood of tragedy.

I was sliding through dirty New Jersey snow, looking for footprints, happy as a rose in sunshine. I got a byline every day. Every morning, I crawled out of my miserable motel bed and sang while I got dressed. I brought doughnuts and cigarettes and dirty jokes wherever I went and when reporters were getting shut out of Hopewell, New Jersey, I was not one of them. I sat over a typewriter in a freezing room, still wearing my coat and hat, and banged out story after story and chased clue after clue. It was as good a serial as you could find on the radio. Thirteen ransom notes and a host of screwy characters, including John Condon, a high school principal, who popped up out of nowhere to offer himself as an intermediary between Lindbergh and the kidnappers. John Condon seemed serious, modest, distraught and I think he was the best con man I ever saw. None of us ever figured out what his long game was. If poor Richard Hauptmann, the kidnapper, had been as clever as John Condon, he wouldn't have got the chair. And if poor Richard Hauptmann hadn't been German, the press wouldn't have tagged him with the nickname "Bruno" and we wouldn't have had to pretend that the two eyewitnesses against him were anything but blind and broke. I could write anything, take up any crazy clue (a scrap of blue fabric in Maryland, a mystery man in Rhode Island), as long as the root of the story was untouched: American hero and wife search for missing baby.

Every suspicion we had of corruption and desperation on the part of the cops and J. Edgar Hoover and the FBI, we kept to ourselves. Lindbergh was untouchable. (Never mind his "America First" speeches, blaming Jews for anti-Semitism. Never mind that famous, boyish grin flashing when he got the Commander Cross of the Order of the German Eagle from Göring in Berlin in 1938, with Hitler's best wishes. And most of all, never mind that just four months before the kidnapping, Lucky Lindy had taken his baby and hidden him in a linen closet while his wife, Anne Morrow Lindbergh, searched the house weeping hysterically. Then he handed her the baby. What a card.)

I believed Lindbergh hired John Condon. I thought Lindbergh killed the baby by accident and built a cover-up with the bravado and precision he was famous for. And when the poor little baby was found, four miles from the house, head staved in and decomposing, poor German Richard Hauptmann didn't have a chance.

I didn't write the story I wanted to and everyone knew it. My boss said to me, Give it up. Go cover Eleanor Roosevelt for a change, her old man's heading to the White House. I didn't say no. Albany was a one-horse town and Eleanor Roosevelt might be dull and pleasant, which is what I'd heard, but I was pretty sure she hadn't killed her own baby and sent an innocent man to fry for it.

She was dull and pleasant for the first five minutes. I sat right next to her in a faded velvet chair, in the old-fashioned drawing room of the Governor's Mansion on Eagle Street, and looked at her cheap, sensible serge dress and flat shoes and thought, Who in the name of Christ has dressed you? I looked closely, to make notes, and then I looked away to be polite. She poured tea and I did notice her beautiful hands and her very plain wedding band, a little loose on her finger. We chatted. We sipped. I made some remarks about Republicans and she laughed, and not politely.

She asked me about the Lindbergh case and I told her about what I'd seen and she shook her head over Lindbergh. I prefer Amelia Earhart, she said. You know, she was a social worker, before she was a pilot. That's not all she was, I thought, but I ate a cookie.

We talked about the great state of New York and the needs of its people and then it was time for dinner and we had a sherry-spiked mushroom soup I can still taste. We ate and talked until late. She told me that her husband believed that the role of government was to help people. I nodded. All people, she said. She told me about Louis Howe, Governor Roosevelt's campaign manager, whom she had come to admire. I didn't at first, she said. She said some people thought he was a Machiavelli. She said he was coarse and direct and deeply, deeply political. But Louis Howe is also, she said, the kindest, most loyal, most decent person I know. When my husband got polio—she put her hand over her mouth. Please don't write that, she said. That is not the kind of thing I wish to discuss, in the newspapers. I made a big show of striking a line. We'll go with Louis Howe and his fine qualities, I said. Now, give me something uplifting, so we go out on a positive note about the governor and his race for the White House.

"The function of democratic living is not to lower standards but to raise those that have been too low."

"That's very good," I said.

She rang a bell and said, Would you care for a sherry? Her eyes were light blue, then dark blue, lake blue. I saw a quick flare, a pilot light of interest come and go.

I put away my notebook and we sat, sipping sherry, listening to opera, until a maid came in and asked if she should get my coat.

I said, Mrs. Roosevelt, I hate to go, but I have a story to file. She said, Don't make me sound like a fool, Miss Hickok. I said that I couldn't if I tried and she said she thought that was the first lie I'd told her. We both stood up and she helped me on with my coat. We looked at each other in their grand, gold-framed mirror and she adjusted my hat. Then she said, We're grown women, both doing our jobs. Call me Eleanor. I smiled all the way home.

We saw each other every week of the campaign and I liked what I saw so much, I offered to cover her full-time for the Associated Press as Roosevelt's race for the White House heated up. My editor liked the pieces and every once in a while he'd say, Your lady's got some good lines. I liked her height and her energy. I liked her long, loose stride and her progressive principles. She insulted conservatives and cowards every time she opened her mouth and I wrote it all down. She smiled when she saw me coming and I did the same. When we had breakfast together, I sometimes took a sausage off her plate.

She called me at the end of October and told me that Franklin's secretary's mother had died. I'd already met Missy LeHand, the governor's executive secretary, his lodestar of competence and tact and likely something more. Dozens of reporters, including me, saw Missy sitting very close to Governor Roosevelt, late at night, rubbing his shoulders. Eleanor said she didn't want to make the trip to Potsdam, New York, with just dear, bereft Missy and Franklin certainly wasn't going to attend that shit storm of weeping, hopeful women (which was not how Eleanor put it). She said, Won't you come with us, Hick? It's quite a long ride, we'll get better acquainted and then we'll tour a power plant. We can go see where they want to put the Saint Lawrence Seaway.

I was between girlfriends and between dogs. I packed my bag.

Before we got on the train, we stopped in a department store, for her to get some handkerchiefs. Only a few heads turned. I said I could use a new scarf. We walked through together and for a minute we linked arms, like lady shoppers with time on their hands. We got her plain linen hankies and I picked up and put down a red silk scarf. Very racy, she said. You should get it. We sat, side by side, in the department store café, which would have been heaven to me when I was growing up, a clean place to eat, drinks brought to you by tidy-looking women, surrounded by silk flowers. I ordered a grilled cheese-and-bacon sandwich and wished they served beer. Eleanor, who liked to pretend she didn't care for anything self-indulgent, had a bowl of split pea soup. It came with oyster crackers and after she had dumped her packet of them into the bowl, she looked to see if I might have some, next to my sandwich.

"Why don't you just ask for some more crackers," I said.

"This is fine. This is what they gave us," she said.

I gave the waitress a little wave and a big smile. When she came by, I asked for three more packets of crackers. Eleanor clasped her hands in irritation and then she turned it on.

"The crackers are so good, miss," Eleanor said. "If it *is* extra, please just put it on our bill."

I said, "No one is going to accuse the future First Lady of chowing down oyster crackers at the expense of the working class."

She did laugh and she put two of the packets back on my plate, unopened.

On the train to Potsdam, Eleanor sat down next to Missy. I pretended to read. She held Missy's hand. Missy said she hated funerals. She said that she didn't like leaving the President for so long and Eleanor smiled. No one can take your place, she said. Eleanor gave Missy the drawing room and we took the sleeping car. I didn't think of Missy again.

Eleanor and I couldn't take our eyes off each other. We pressed knees. We patted arms. We shared our sandwiches. We shared an apple and a bunch of grapes and we took turns, plucking the grapes off the stem. We talked and talked in her sleeping compartment and at about ten o'clock at night, I realized that she wasn't going to be putting on a nightgown, or whatever she wore at night. I had brought my navy-blue Sulka pajamas, classy and not creepy, in my overnight bag, but I didn't want to take them out, uninvited. Navy-blue Sulka pajamas, worn by the Duke of Windsor and picked out by Wallis Simpson, were in every fashion magazine.

I'd met Wallis Simpson. Twice. She wasn't pretty. She was a skinny roughhouser from a shitbox Southern town but she had done a phenomenal job of remaking herself, vanquishing good-looking rivals, and turning a genial, not stupid, sort of spineless royal into her love-slave. Like a lot of rich people, she liked the Nazis more than she liked Democrats and she was famous for kissing up and kicking down. She worried that people would see who she'd been: the homely daughter of a Baltimore flour salesman with lots of charm and lots of unpaid bills. She did away with the charm and the debts and she did, in her awful way, offer hope to those of us who were not conventional beauties.

Eleanor and I were not conventional beauties. That's what we'd say and we'd laugh, to underscore *conventional,* as if maybe we were some other kind. But the pictures of Eleanor floating in yards of white on her wedding day are so pretty, her sweet face crowned with her lovely dark-gold hair and handfuls of lilies, you'd have to think that the terrible photos of her later on must have all been taken by Republicans. Later, when I did complain about the magazine photos, Eleanor would fan through the worst of them and sigh. She said, Dearest, when one has buck teeth and a weak chin, one can hardly blame the photographer. But I did. I also hated my photos (You have to keep your arm at least six inches *away* from your body, a friend of Eleanor's told me, so you're not all bulk) but Eleanor didn't like vanity and I pretended to grow out of it.

On the train, we sipped sherry as the sun set and watched the world pass by in yellow and pink sunset, fields and lakes, small houses with scrub yards, washing hung up, tall, narrow trees, lightless and struggling, and at two A.M., at the right time, on the night train, we cried for each other.

"My mother," she said, "was exceptionally beautiful. She was famous for it. And she found me . . . disappointing. I was plain, you see, and shy, and my mother loved parties, loved gaiety. I was a serious little thing, I'm afraid."

I pressed her hand.

"My father," she said, taking back her hand, "thought I was a miracle from heaven. He praised everything I did. He encouraged bravery and self-reliance. He pushed me to excel and to speak my mind."

She looked down.

"I'm not as good at that as I should be. But he wanted me to be a strong person, standing on my own two feet. He always did. He had his own difficulties, unfortunately."

I said that rich or poor, people struggled with their demons and then I added that what I really meant was, people struggle and it's better to be rich.

Eleanor looked out the window.

"When I was quite a little girl, two and a half, my parents, and my nurse, a wonderful girl, and my Aunt Tissie, we all sailed to Europe."

She ran her finger down the misty window.

"Once upon a time," I said.

"Oh, you're exactly right. Once upon a time, a very small, plain girl with too many teeth and a great white bow got on a great big boat, with her beautiful mother, her dashing father, her kind-hearted nursemaid, and her fun-loving Aunt Tissie. They all boarded the *Britannic* with more boxes and trunks and suitcases than you can imagine. The little girl got to keep her doll in a hatbox. They were off to see the Continent. Of Europe."

"I've never been to Europe," I said. Take me.

"You would love London," she said. "I still have lots of friends there. School friends."

We both contemplated English schoolgirls and she blushed.

"On the very first day of the little girl's trip, the fog came in. It blew across the ocean and lay on top of everything. Have you ever been fogged in? It's unpleasant."

"I'm from South Dakota," I said. "Anything that's not dirt appeals to me."

"Well, the fog was very thick. On deck, I had trouble finding my toast. I still remember," she said. "Cinnamon toast."

She smiled, painfully.

"Suddenly, people were screaming and running past the little girl. Children were screaming. The little girl saw a fountain of blood flying up in the air and landing on the deck, spattering the tea table. The little girl had no idea what was happening. As it turned out, it was a steamer ramming into us. A big man, bigger than her father, picked her up and held her close. She could smell the salt on his blue jacket and she could see the stiff, shiny quills of his short blond hair. Her beautiful mama and her dashing father and her kindhearted nursemaid and her wonderful Aunt Tissie were all standing in a little white boat far below, calling for her. They wanted the man in the blue jacket to throw the little girl down into the boat. Her father said that he would catch her, he promised he would catch her, but the little girl could see that with all the screaming and the blood and the fog, the man in the blue jacket would drop her and no one would be able to catch her. The little girl grabbed at the man's buttons. She grabbed at his hair. The man pulled the little girl's fingers loose, pushing them back so she couldn't hold on to him anymore. He held her by the waist and dropped her like a stone. She fell very, very slowly into her father's arms. She was safe. She knew she was safe but, according to everyone, she cried for days afterward. Her beautiful mama said that the crash was not that bad but the little girl remembered the screams and the cries for help and the bleeding children for the rest of her life. A little boy lost his arm. And, I absolutely hate being on board a ship," she said.

I will never take you on a cruise, I thought.

Eleanor asked me to tell her a once-upon-a-time story from my childhood. I said, Let me think.

People like when their griefs balance, when the sufferings can share the same stage. My heartache, your heartache. My illness, your illness. Not my broken arm, your mass murder. I fold up my jacket and put it on my shoulder and I sit up straight, and if she stretches out, she can rest her head on me.

I was thirteen years old. My father bent over me, one hand on my shoulder, the other steadying himself on the slats. He pressed me hard from behind, up against the skinny fence between our house and the railroad yard. His suspenders slapped against my back, light and rhythmic. They didn't hurt. I bunched my school dress up between my stomach and the splintering wood and held on tight to the pickets, so I didn't lose my balance and slide back in the hard dirt toward him. I arced way away from him but not enough and there was pain in my private parts, where it felt like he was taking a chisel to me, time after time. I watched crows vee across the sky, to take my mind off everything. My father wiped himself off with his shirttail and buttoned up. We both watched the crows.

I straightened my dress and socks and I shook the dirt off my shoes. It would be so good if it was him that died and my mother that had got better. Myrtle and Ruby and I would stay with my mother and we'd all start again someplace better than Bowdle, South Dakota, and its flat, treeless misery. We'd go back in time to Milbank, which was not so bad, or way back to Elgin, which was before Myrtle was born and had water and green leaves, and the barbershop and Mama being a seamstress, so Ruby and I each had a Sunday dress and a school dress and play clothes too. Now, wherever we'd be, it'd be just the four of us, sitting around a table with an oilcloth on it and four plates and forks and real napkins and my mother humming, dishing out rabbit stew. Ruby hands around the monkey bread and Myrtle is remade, in my imagination, into a nice little girl. The sky is blue and white, the orange sun dropping, all of our chores done, the one pleasant hour in a South Dakota summer day.

My father passed his hand over my mouth, just as a reminder, and I smelled the chickenshit and milk on his hand. He tapped me on the leg, to show me where blood was trickling down my legs. He took out his bandanna from his pocket and tucked it into my hand and he walked back to the house, a little hitch in his gait. I stayed by the fence for a while, smoothing my dress from where I crushed it against the fence, and then I went to the pump and gave it a few, cleaning myself off from the waist down until I was soaking. I was clean. I hid the bandanna under a rock.

I dawdled, the way I did. There was nothing to hurry for, no better place I could get to, and when I finally went in, still dripping water into my shoes, Myrtle was sitting in my mother's rocker, the cushion back on the seat, pulling a splinter out of her foot. Ruby sat on the floor, twisting herself into a little knot. My father's hat was gone and a woman I'd never seen before was sweeping our kitchen floor.

"I'm Miz Min," she said.

My little sisters lowered their eyes.

"Your daddy's gone to be a traveling salesman now and I'm here to keep things going."

I said, "What about the butter-making? Isn't he going to make butter anymore?"

Miz Min looked at me. I don't think it occurred to her that we'd talk. She opened the kitchen door and spat her tobacco outside.

"You hear me? Your daddy's a traveling salesman now. He'll be home at the end of the week. He's a drummer, now." She put her hands on her hips. "You gonna mind me."

I walked to our room, trying to show gumption. The little girls followed me. They watched me dry myself off on the bottom of my mother's quilt and they waited until I was done. It was still light out but I took off my shoes and got into our bed and the girls did the same. As vicious as Myrtle could be in her sleep—foot in your eye, elbow right in the kidney—I let her stay on my right side, her hair fanning over me, and Ruby curled up like a baby on my left, her fat little hands around my neck.

We'd already lived through the dark night of my mother's stroke a week ago, coming right after laundry day, the worst day of the week and as hot a wet hell as you can imagine. My father'd come into our bedroom late at night, pulling me up out of our bed, telling me to hurry and get dressed, just like he had me walk to the store for flour or oats when we ran out, except that it was pitch-dark and he was talking in what we called his friendly way, meaning that he wasn't likely to pull a stave out of the butter keg and whip me or Ruby or Myrtle black and blue right then.

He said, "Your mother's not well."

He shoved me down the hall and opened the door to their room. I'd never been in their room when they were both in it. I helped my mother out, when I had to, with the basin and pitcher and bringing her the commode. Twice, she got bronchitis and last year a neighbor lady sent us hog stew and my mother got so sick on it, she puked until nothing more came up and still she was twisting and turning on the floor. I helped too after Ruby was born, helped my mother to get right and feed Ruby, because the visiting nurse had come and gone in no time. My mother lay back on the pillow and I pulled her breast into the baby's mouth, rolling the milk down and squeezing and flicking Ruby's cheeks to suck. When Ruby and I were playing and I was a little too rough on her and she said why was I doing her like that, sometimes I said, I am your true mama and what I say goes.

My father and I stood on either side of the bed in their small, hot room, the paper shade flapping against the one window. Their quilt was on the floor. He looked at my mother and at me and he pushed me toward the bed.

"Lorena's here," he said.

Her chest was heaving, her gray cracked feet kicked at nothing. But she did breathe. Her mouth opened ragged and wet against the pillow and spit ran out, wetting the ends of her gray braid, and I kept my eyes on the rattling shade and thought, You can beat me till hell freezes over and still, I am not gonna take care of her. Will not, no more than she took care of me these last years. My father beat us, but Ruby had sweetness and Myrtle was little and I was the oldest, so, mostly me. When I played follow-the-leader with the two of them in the barn, and they slipped on the ladder and skinned their knees, I comforted them and thought, That's nothing to what I go through and you do not.

My mother lived for peace. When my father whipped our puppy for peeing on the rug, my mother covered her face with her apron until he was done, and she swept the puppy's body out to the ditch. When he slung our kitten against the side of the barn, a full five times, my mother stood by the road, with her hat and coat on, as if she were about to leave him, and she watched him toss its little gold body in the weeds. Ruby and I wrapped it up, after school, in a scrap of crochet my mother handed me (finger on her lips, back of the kitchen) and I sang "Blessed Assurance."

Blessed assurance, Jesus is mine!
Oh, what a foretaste of glory divine!
Heir of salvation, purchase of God,
Born of His Spirit, washed in His blood.

And Ruby, who couldn't carry a tune in a bucket, belted it out beside me. Myrtle, who had more of my father than my mother in her, poked the dead cat with a stick, mumbling, until we'd sung all four verses and buried the little thing properly. We came back in and my mother gave us molasses on bread heels and she put her finger to her lips again, watching road.

My mother wanted peace when she was living and peace when she was dying. She cried out, looking up at the ceiling, Mother of God, let me go. I walked as far around her bed as I could and opened the window to give her some air. I waved the shade, to make a fan for her. I had to empty the commode and walked downstairs with it, my face pulled in from the black, terrible sea in the bowl, and the ugly shapes in it lapped up to the edge and I tried to keep my fingers and shoes from being splashed with it. It stank and I emptied it and washed it out and washed it again, and somehow the porcelain bowl still stank. Where I poured it out, nothing would ever grow. I washed my hands at the pump, with a handful of Borax. I moved as slow as I dared, back up the stairs, to turn her over, trying to be careful of the purple bruises blossoming up and down her knobby spine, to flip the sheet, to close the window now that dust was coming onto her, to give her some water from the teacup and clean up when she couldn't keep even the water down. I moved too slow and she rose a little and grabbed my sleeve.

"Oh, Jesus, it hurts," she said and fell back, pulling on me, until I was down beside her on the bed. I wiggled toward the floor, away from the stink, and she put her hand in my hair and held on.

"Ain't you got the curls," she said.

She gasped and I sat up. She gasped again and let go.

"Never mind," she said. "You scared?"

I was scared. I tried not to inhale, to not catch what she had. She would die and I would die next.

My mother turned her face away from the window. The shade was broken. I hung one of her dresses over the rod and she nodded. She yawned and I said, hopefully, You tired, Mama? You want to take a little rest? She shook her head and yawned again and I could see into her mouth, her thick tongue, her bright red gums, the spaces where she'd lost her teeth. (Have a baby, lose a tooth, everyone said.) She stank to high heaven and I went to open the window. Her eyes rolled back in her head and she opened her mouth wide, the veins in her neck popping, as if to scream, and she settled down suddenly, easing into the pillow. A little blood ran out of her mouth and I ran down the stairs, running over Ruby, who grabbed at my legs, kicking Myrtle to one side.

My father'd slept on the kitchen floor with two blankets under his back and the rocker cushion for a pillow and he'd left them in a pile.

I saw him by the fence and ran over. I told him my mother was bleeding out her mouth. He asked if she was still talking and I said that we spoke just a minute ago.

"She ain't dying, then. You go back up. Wipe her mouth with water. Folks get dry."

He took a drink from his flask and handed it over.

"You can give her this."

I didn't ask when would he come upstairs or when could I stop sitting with her.

I spooned out whiskey for her until the flask was empty.

"Pa says you ain't dying," I said.

She lifted her chin.

I pulled the sheet up to her shoulders and she pushed it away, wincing.

"I'm gonna go," I said. "Just downstairs."

She waved her hand sideways.

I slept in until the sunlight beat on my face. The little girls were scattered, out of the house. My father was in the kitchen with the minister and an older lady.

"Lorena," my father said and I bobbed down, to show respect.

The minister said, Shall we pray, and my father let his head drop forward, like an old horse, waiting for the bit, and I did the same. The minister said Jesus and Our Lord and he said my mother's name. He said Anna Hickok, mother of Lorena, Rose, and Myrtle, beloved wife of Addison Hickok and that's how I knew. I could hear the girls playing down the road. I sighed and my father tightened his grip on my hand and rubbed my knuckle-bones together, to warn me.

The minister's voice died down and I said, I oughta look after the girls, and I broke away.

I went down by the fence. Ruby was still crying and Myrtle was her usual wild-dog self.

"It's gonna be all right," I said.

"Not, it will not," Myrtle said.

I put Ruby up on my shoulder and dragged Myrtle down the path. We sat in the barn, napping in the shade and playing hop-scotch with an old horseshoe, until it was almost dark. I figured whichever neighbors could put something together would be bringing us a bread or a chess pie or some potato and beans before nightfall. I was right and the four of us sat down and ate a dinner like we hadn't had in a year and my father didn't smack anyone's hand away from anything. Ruby said, God bless Mama, and the three of us nodded. That was my mother's funeral.

My father came home the last Friday in August, in the tight salesman's suit and greasy celluloid collar Miz Min made him buy. The suit made him look cheap, which he was, and dishonest, which he was not, not in the business way. He set his brown bowler on the sideboard and his wrinkled jacket on the back of the rocker and he stretched his neck from side to side. He nodded to Miz Min. She dusted off a chair for him and told us to sit by her. My father said that Ruby was going to live with an uncle on my mother's side, in Wisconsin. "Good people," he said and Miz Min shrugged. She didn't give a fiddler's fuck if they were good people or not. Ruby was the sweet and pretty one, my father's favorite, if he had one, and to have her gone would be a relief for Miz Min, I think.

Myrtle was hell on two feet, but she was sly and only six and they'd keep Myrtle with them for a while longer, until she gave them cause.

I was stubborn trouble at home, and almost a woman. I had a nice singing voice and when things were not too bad, my father took me to church and sat in the front pew (like a paying customer, he said) and made sure I got a solo. I could see the way Miz Min would see it.

My father got down a cardboard box from his closet and said that there were people in town, plenty of them, looking for a "hired girl." One dollar a week, he said. Maybe more. Plus meals. Not too bad and you can keep going to school. He said that surely I could clean a house and we both snorted because I never did a lick of housework after my mother got sick, and he knew it. He beat me every day the week before she passed and all it got him was shrunken trousers and stew so salty and soapy, he let us put it in a pan behind the house and watch to see what kind of brave gophers might come for it. I didn't think Miz Min would have let us watch what happened to the stew.

She gave Myrtle a little tap on the fanny, to show that Myrtle needed to be minding Miz Min for real now, and she said to me that since the three of them would be moving on, she advised me to do the same.

She said, "If you can help it, don't clump around. And smile. People like it when a girl smiles."

I went to our room and my father followed me in. He put a cardboard box on the bed. This is for your things, he said. He put in my mother's hairbrush. Use it, he said. I folded up every bit of clothing I had, my mother's shoes, and the last of her lily-of-the-valley soap, which she'd used, sliver by sliver, since I was a little girl. I hugged Ruby hard, and we hid our faces in each other's shoulders, trying not to give way. I waved to Myrtle, who lifted her hand. My father walked me to the door and opened it.

I walked down the road and around the first bend, to where they couldn't see me. I knew this road like a conductor knows the tracks. It was past six o'clock on a Friday night in August. The sky was still bright blue, the edge of the trees just a hair darker. Town traffic was done. Farmers were done. I could have stood or slept right in the middle of the road and never seen a soul.

I slept under a cottonwood and woke up with my arms around my box. I had nowhere to go but Lottie Miller's house, four miles away. Lottie was the other smart girl in our school. We sat together at lunch for three years in a row. I got to sit with Lottie for twenty minutes at a time, holding her hand, breathing her in. Once I saw I could get my foot in the door with Lottie, I made a real effort. I brushed my hair and chewed mint on the way to school. Her mother sometimes came by to walk her home from school and I always gave her a big Hello, Mrs. Miller and she smiled. Lottie's father was one of the shopkeepers who used to yell at Myrtle.

I spit on my shirtsleeve to wipe my face and dragged the hairbrush through my hair. I tied it all back with my hair ribbon and I hoped that even if I looked like a fool or a hobo, my wish to please the Millers would please them.

I sat on the Millers' back porch for about an hour, until I saw Lottie's mother, moving around the kitchen in her housedress. She gasped when she saw me. She managed, without being unkind, to get me to rinse off in the hip bath, while she stood guard at the back door. She asked me if my mother and father knew where I was and I told her that my father had told me to go get a job and my mother died three weeks ago. I smiled at every question, to show how willing and pleasant I was.

I should have hidden myself under the piece of linen Lottie's mother handed me, but there was a breeze. It came through the back door, touching me on my chest and neck and between my legs. Water ran from my hair down my back, to my feet. I shook my hair so it sprayed water around me. It was heaven. I had never been lovely in all my conscious life but I knew right then, standing barefoot on the rag rug on top of the linoleum, that I was clean, and young and damp and that that was a kind of lovely. Lottie's mother turned her back right away.

I patted myself dry slowly, feeling my skin through the old sheet. I dried my toes and all of my parts. I held the sheet like a shawl and shimmied it up and down my back. I put on my only underclothes and my blue blouse and my better skirt and my mother's shoes. I could see Mrs. Miller had hoped that a decent bath and doing my hair in braids would make me more like Lottie. I had hoped so too. I knew we had a problem.

I ate on the back porch at supper, so as not to disturb Mr. Miller, who worked long hours. I put myself fully in the hands of Mrs. Miller, just to pretend that I was a girl like Lottie, floating along in a loving stream, cared for and watched over. I prayed that Lottie's mother might take me in. I left no crumbs. I cleaned my shoes every day. I only drank water and I never asked for seconds, so no one would think I'd be any kind of burden on the Miller household. In the evenings, I swept out the kitchen and sat on the back porch, still as a bucket, waiting until Lottie gave me the high sign to run up to her room. I was thirteen years old and if I was going to hell, or the poorhouse, or was forced to sell myself in downtown Pierre, like one of the older girls at school had said could happen, I was gonna have a holiday first.

Lottie and I read poetry aloud. We found Mrs. Miller's Ouija board in the attic and I made it say that I would go far and Lottie would marry a rich and handsome fellow. I teased Lottie about her future husband, hoping it might lead to us playing Honeymoon, which we'd played before, on a rainy afternoon, when the road to my house was washing out and Rose and Myrtle had stayed with our teacher. We were getting ready for Honeymoon (Lottie with a pillowcase over her head, like a scarf, to signify train travel and me, the groom, with a cardigan buttoned over my blouse). Lottie's mother came in and stood in the doorway. She said we were too loud and I was banished to the sleeping porch. I folded up the quilt every morning and swept the porch too, to show some more of my goodness. On the fourth day of the only holiday I'd ever had, Lottie's mother woke me up early. Mr. Miller had already gone and Lottie was still sleeping. She took my hand and brought me into her bedroom. She gave me a white slip and one of her own dresses. She brushed my hair and clipped it back with a pair of enamel slides, which was pretty much tying a ribbon on a side of beef, but I let her. She gave me a pair of Lottie's embroidered anklets and we both tried to make something of my mother's shoes, which were close to falling apart.

"I wish we wore the same size," she said. "Honest to goodness, I'd give you my own."

"I know you would," I said. "You are the kindest person I've ever known. Ain't nobody like you."

"Isn't." Lottie's mother sighed. "Thank you."

When Eleanor woke up, I said that I could tell her my story now, if she wanted, and she said she did. I said we'd been poor most of my life (we had two good years in Wisconsin, I said, but I don't remember them very well), and even worse, we were poor in South Dakota. I said that my father had been brutal to me and my sisters and that my mother died when I was thirteen and I had nursed her as best I could.

"It must have meant so much to your mother, having you there," Eleanor said.

"I hope so."

I told her that I'd lost track of my two little sisters and I told her a funny story about me and Ruby making kites out of newspaper, when we were little. I told her about playing Uncle Tom's Cabin and I told her I'd worked as a hired girl for a while, mopping the floor and burning the brownies. I told her about Mrs. Miller's kindness.

"I'm not much of a housekeeper," I said.

"Nor am I," she said. "I wasn't raised to do it. I must say, I admire women who have domestic skills."

I said I admired people who could kill, skin, and cook a rabbit but I didn't want to do what they did.

Eleanor patted my shoulder and walked out of our compartment. She came back, wearing a fresh blouse and fresh lipstick (My daughter makes me, she said), carrying a tray of coffee, orange juice, and rolls. Eleanor said that she'd meet Missy and go with her to the funeral. You needn't, she said, meaning I shouldn't. I thought I could write a pretty hot story about the governor's wife and mistress attending the funeral of the mistress's mother, but then I'd have no more Eleanor and no ride home.

I said I'd find myself a diner and sit there until the five-o'clock train whistled. We parted at the station and I watched her go.

To this day, I love a diner. I tucked two dollars under the sugar bowl so the one waitress, a tall, pretty redhead with freckles head to foot, would pour me coffee all day. At lunchtime, a few salesmen came in and at three o'clock we got some mothers and their lucky, well-fed children. A dark, chunky girl and a slim, ratty blonde sat in the booth in front of me, sharing a Moxie, folding their straw wrappers into a chain. The blonde said if she never cleaned another toilet again, it'd be too soon. The dark girl sighed and they slipped off their shoes.

My people, the hired girls.

I didn't tell Eleanor much. I didn't tell her that I had cried into my sleeve when Mrs. Miller brought me to the gate of a good-sized house. We will all miss you, she said, but this really is a decent job and you can still go to school. She had smoothed back my hair one more time and she kissed me on the forehead, which I felt for days after. I told her straight out that I wasn't up to snuff, that I'd done my best to fool her with the sweeping and wiping my shoes but I hadn't ever done laundry beyond diapers or made a meal or looked after anyone except Ruby and Myrtle and what I'd done with them wasn't exactly a recommendation. Lottie's mother looked to the right and the left and she whispered that it was no matter; the O'Neills couldn't get anyone better, because of their papish ways.

There was a small Catholic church fifty miles away and the Klan had ridden through a few of the bigger towns, was what I heard, but I hadn't heard that anyone had burned a cross in front of the church or hurt the people at the Chinese laundry. And, still, the reason the O'Neills would take me was that the better class of hired girl—neat, pleasant, cheerful, good with a peeler and a dust mop—wouldn't work for Irish people. I couldn't do a goddamn thing but make porridge and wash a baby's diapers until they didn't stink and still they would have me. One dollar a week.

The O'Neills were easy. They were not nicer than Mrs. Miller, who I see now was a motivated seller, but they were filled with confidence and enough money, from where I stood, and they loved each other, which astonished me. The first time Charley O'Neill raised his hand to his wife, I flinched. He tucked a brown-edged daisy from the yard behind her ear and she kissed his hand. Their little girl, giddy with all the love, pressed her face to Mrs. O'Neill's breast and I thought, Oh, who *are* you people? I loved them, the way girls today love their movie stars. I got up early, to make breakfast for little Lucille, and for baby Brendan. Mrs. O'Neill came down to supervise, looking tousled and charming, like a Gibson girl at dawn. I fed the kids and cleaned the baby's diaper. I scoured the pot and ran out the door to school, eating my toast or Brendan's teething biscuit. When Miss West dismissed us, I tore ass back to the O'Neills', to get dinner started and keep up with the diapers. Sometimes Lottie ran part of the way with me and when I turned off for the O'Neills', she waved, warmly, and I waved back, hard as I could. Lottie was too kind to take up entirely with another girl but I did see her look with interest at Addie Long, at lunchtime.

I was, just as I'd said, not much good as a hired girl. It turned out that I was good enough company for Mrs. O'Neill. She was from far-off Boston, which accounted for her odd accent and her occasional cigarette, even though she was not a bad woman. She told me that one October afternoon, while she leafed through a magazine and I rocked both the kids. I laughed and I told her that smoking a cigarette was not my idea of a bad woman. She said that she was surprised that a young girl like me had any idea of what a bad woman even was. I said, Oh, I did, for sure, and she shook her head. I'll get some rest myself, she said and left me rocking the baby carriage and the bassinet, in the shade. I washed her intimate things, I cleaned her babies' bottoms, and I scrubbed every dirty thing I came across. I didn't do any of it well, but I made an effort, as Mrs. O'Neill often said, and it was better than having to live in Bowdle, South Dakota, and clean house all day herself. I used to be a secretary, she said.

I was bathing the kids in the hip bath, in the kitchen, letting the baby blow bubbles and letting Lucille splash all over. Mrs. O'Neill was keeping an eye on us and making remarks about the magazine recipe for brownies and whether or not either one of us could produce a tray of them with her temperamental oven. We both heard the knock on the front door. It was low-class for her to answer the door herself but I was soaked and barefoot and that was worse. She looked at my feet and went to the door. I laid the baby on the wet floor and put on my socks and shoes. I pushed back my hair and dried my face and hands. I heard my father's voice and I sat back down on the floor, with Lucille and Baby Bren in my lap. Mrs. O'Neill came in, and her voice shook a little.

She'd never had a man in the house without Mr. O'Neill around and I knew she'd never met a man like my father. I left your father in the parlor, she said. No, ma'am, my father said, right behind her. He looked down at the naked babies and me and I wrapped them both up and handed them to Mrs. O'Neill, who stood beside me. Mrs. O'Neill was a pretty Boston rosebud and she would not be saving me from Addison Hickok. Lorena is like a member of the family, she said. She's such a help.

My father nodded. He said it was best that I move with him and Myrtle and Miz Min to Aberdeen. He said that whatever I was doing for this family, I could do for another. He said they was starting over in Aberdeen and could use my wages. To Mrs. O'Neill he said, Thank you for putting up with Lorena. I stood in my little room until he called my name. I got my cardboard box and went back to the kitchen, where Mrs. O'Neill gave me a hug, and pressed fifty cents into my hand on the sly. The two kids waved goodbye from the floor. On the way out the door, I stole a stamp from Mr. O'Neill's desk, to send a note to Ruby in Wisconsin, about us heading for Aberdeen, which I did never get to. Miz Min was waiting with the wagon, and Myrtle lay in the back, sprawled across two suitcases. I climbed in back and Myrtle kicked at me, to keep me from getting comfortable. As it was getting dark, we pulled up in front of an old farm. Men were sitting on benches in the front and smoke curled up from their pipes and a small campfire. My father said, This here's your stop. I'll hold on to your pay. Miz Min didn't say a word and Myrtle stuck out her tongue, which was the last time I ever saw her.

An old lady opened the door.

"I'm Mrs. Cotter. You're Lorena. Your father says you can cook. You'll be the cook," she said.

"I guess so," I said.

I saw Mrs. Cotter take my measure, rawboned and broad-shouldered in a made-over dress. People had been sizing me up for a year. They'd been looking hard.

"You don't look sneaky," she said.

"No, ma'am, I'm a straight shooter."

"Well, what choice do you have," she said. "Looking like you do."

She tossed me a couple of peanuts from an open sack on the floor.

"I'll pay a dollar a week, you can sleep in the kitchen, and no nocturnal visitation, you know what I'm saying?"

"I'm not expecting any visitors," I said.

I slept on a bedroll in the kitchen, cooking for the threshers for three weeks. All the farmers had got together to hire threshers. Two boys my age had come to the threshing with their uncle. They said the settling up at the end was usually more of a party than anything else. The men sat at long tables, drinking, and the farmers with single daughters made small talk with the men who'd stood out as hard workers.

"It's a big party," Bernie said. "You can get yourself a husband."
His brother laughed and so did I.

"You can get yourself a beer," Jim said.

It was bad weather for weeks, and the settling up seemed likely to
never come. The farmers' wives and daughters were cooking over-
time. I was blistered and dirty with burns striped to my elbow. I
learned how to cook for a crowd. The boys sat by the fire with me
most nights while I lay down near the stove because my feet
couldn't take it anymore. Bernie said he heard that this settling up
was going to be ugly. He said it didn't look like payday was going
to come for them. I said their uncle didn't seem to be looking out
for them and Bernie said, Uncle, my white ass. Bernie said they
might hitch a ride out on the lumber wagon when it came by tomorrow before breakfast. Jim said, Hell yes, they might, and he
showed me a red wool sock with three silver dollars in it.

"Come on, Hick," Bernie said. "Come with. Ain't nothing good
gonna happen to you here."

I stretched out on the floor, not minding the soot or the em-
bers. I was almighty tired and I was as dirty as the boys.

"Go on and take something," Jim said. "We'll be lookout."

I crept down the hall to the old man's desk. I gathered myself.
I wiped my hands on my skirt and went drawer by drawer through
his big oak desk. I found a little drawer, shaped like a cube and
running the whole of the desk from front to back, hidden under a
pretty square of bird's-eye maple. I held up two silver dollars and
the boys whooped, quietly. I felt that great tide inside, danger and
joy rising and falling, and I grabbed Mrs. Cotter's gray felt church
hat and their best bread knife and put them both in my cardboard
box.

The boys and I walked down to the bend and we waited until the lumber wagon came in and then drove out, slowing a bit as it came to the cottonwood we hid behind. The lumberman said, So, three of you, not two. That's another dollar. The boys looked at me and I gave the man one of my dollars. We rode, like brothers and sister, to the train station, and the boys shook my hand. They lit out for better times in Oregon and I made up my mind, as we stood in the train yard, that it was me for Chicago with jobs and schools and my mother's sister, my Aunt Ella.

The trainman called and I held on to my box and my ticket. I fixed the gray hat so I could pass for sixteen. My father ran onto the train, sweating and hatless, yelling at me to come back and do my job. Come run the house. He said Mrs. Cotter told him I'd run off and he said I was on the road to ruin. I stayed in my seat. He said he washed his hands of me. I said that we were even, that I washed my hands of him too. It should have been that he admired my spine and my spunk, but he slapped me across the face and knocked my new hat off. I pressed myself against the window, gripping the box so hard, I put my fingers through it and felt the knife handle. I wrapped my fingers around it and let him see. One couple looked at me and I mimed drinking from a bottle and they shook their heads and I thought, You people will not see me dragged off this train. I held on to the wicker seat until the train began to move and my father jumped off.

Eleanor fell asleep in Oneida.

At dawn, she kissed me on the forehead. You are a wonderful storyteller, she said. She left me to wash up and came back, armored, in another fresh blouse and a stiff blue jacket.

"Like Boadicea," I said, showing off. "Queen of the Iceni."

"Oh yes," she said. "Great warrior. Go on with the story."

She fixed my collar.

"And do spruce up a little," Eleanor said.

Churchill said (to me, in fact), Criticism is like pain. It's not fun but if it doesn't hurt, no one pays attention.

Brother and Sister in One Body

....

I said to Eleanor, My own education began on the train to Chicago. I described the short man in a loud checked suit, walking past me, his manicured hand brushing the back of my seat, steadying himself and rolling with the train. He pushed back his boater and patted his face with a white handkerchief.

He said: Ladies and Gentlemen, I am Lucius P. Wilson.

He gave his ballyhoo and I loved every long, unlikely, and ridiculous sentence.

He said, "Let me introduce you to the seventh, eighth, and ninth Wonders of the World. You may not have expected to find us here in Lake Preston, in Plankinton, in Groton and Brookings, making our magnificent way to Minn-ee-sot-a, by golly, land of a thousand lakes, land of beautiful Indian maidens and their fearsome bucks, culminating in one of our biggest shows ever with the lucky folks of Red Wing, who have begged us, by letter and telegram to return to them with our grand and formidable elephants who have adopted Kiki, our adorable baby hippo, straight from the mud baths of Africa. Our Lipizzaner horses, led by the maestro Tip McCarthy, the greatest horseman of this century, bar none, are in our show under the banner of Showalter's Spectacular Pyrotechnic Pageant. We've got shows and acts for everyone. Bring the old folks and let them gaze with rare delight upon the Forestina Sisters, those queens of the air, with their amazing acrobatics. Husbands, bring your wives. Ladies, bring the menfolk, and you can all enjoy our show of the Golden Orient, starring a bevy of beauties never seen before. Culture, uplift, and that ain't all. . . ."

"Whatcha think, girlie?" he said. "Gonna get your ma and pa to bring you and the rest of the clan to see us in Brookings? That's our last stop here in sunny South Dakota."

I told him I didn't have parents and I was headed for Chicago.

"No parents," he said. "How you getting by?"

I told him, a little stiffly, that I got by and he waved a hand at me.

"I'm not asking about your general welfare. You look like a big, smart girl. I figure you know your stuff, I bet you know how to take shorthand—"

I nodded. Mrs. O'Neill had an old book of the Pitman system from when she'd been a secretary and when Mr. O'Neill worked late, and the babies were asleep, we did practice together. I could write a short letter.

"And you look to me to be eighteen, which you would have to be to take me up on the offer I am making you now, to join Showalter's Show of Shows, the Étoile du Nord Traveling Circus, of which I am only a humble representative and the advance man, Lucius P. Wilson."

He made a little bow. I bobbed down and did not say, I am almost fourteen years old and I got one dollar in my pocket.

"Am I right about you? You got a head for figures and you can read and write real well and, can you type, sister?"

I said I could, which was a lie, but I had seen pictures of people using typewriters and I knew my alphabet and I was a demon speller.

"I am a demon speller," I said.

"I'm never wrong," Mr. Wilson said. "You got a hairbrush or something like it?"

I put my hand up automatically, and I lowered it. I was being eighteen now. I knew shorthand and I could type now. I was a valuable commodity and this was a man with thinning blond hair and a sharp suit with grease spots on the lapel.

"I can smarten up," I said.

He grinned at me. "All right. Can you lose the hat? Smile a little, that'll be swell. If you just can't and folks ask you why you look so goddamn downhearted, you say your mother was Melina, the Lion Queen, and she was mauled to death only last week by one of her own tigers. Oh, looky here, ladies and gentlemen," he said. "*That's* a smile."

We got out at Tyndall, which was a bigger town than Bowdle, bigger than Aberdeen and therefore, to me, a proper city. A man in a Model T drove us to the edge of a wide brown field, spread out for acres and flat as a tabletop. We got out.

I saw pennants and gold-fringed banners being hoisted up, huge white canvas squares, each the size of a roof, lying on the ground, being pulled up by men in undershirts and loose green pants and high work boots. Yards of dirty rope, like giant garter snakes, lay coiled everywhere. A blond woman in a man's jacket and dirty white tights and white boots led two dusty palomino horses across the field. A pair of dark-haired girls walked past with belts of gold fringe around their waists and gold clips shining in their hair, each with a monkey in a gold fringe vest, sitting on her shoulder, screaming while the girls walked and talked. Men unloaded horses, dogs, pigs, and an elephant, red-eyed and slow. A man in overalls fed the elephant handfuls of hay as they walked together. More men wrestled with canvas tents, wires, and pulleys. It was like the inside of a grand clock, sweat and swearing making the gears go round. Red and blue wagons lined the perimeter, their steps thrown down, their shutters closed against the heat. I smelled overcooked vegetables and frying meat, the smell of a farm dinner. I must have looked orphaned. Lucius poked me.

"We can go by the cookhouse later," he said. "But you gotta start work today. I'm behind."

He hit me on the fanny and I took no notice. We walked straight to his wagon, which was two rooms with a narrow door between them.

"This here is reception," he said. "Someone comes, you knock on my door and you say, Mr. Wilson, and you tell me who it is and I come out."

I sat down on one of the chairs, with my hands in my lap, pulling on the brim of my hat. Mr. Wilson took my hat away from me.

"I'm burning this," he said.

We worked in the reception room all afternoon. I sorted papers, filed receipts and bills, and wrote down the names of all the town officials and businessmen and the police officers of every town we'd be going to. He said that he was glad to have a smart and serious girl in the office and that he felt sure there was nothing about me or my person that was going to bring drama or lunacy to Showalter's, for which he personally would be grateful.

I said, "You mean you didn't bring me here to be in the cooch show?"

"Good one," he said.

He said I had no cause to worry, no one was going to let me actually handle money. He said I was going to live in a wagon with two other girls and to not make trouble.

"I'll make an effort," I said. I liked being eighteen.

We ate our fried beef pies in the reception area. Men were still working outside by electric light. He said I'd be bunking with Betsy the Lobster Girl, who was a good girl who got tired of bunking with her parents, the Lobster Man and Lady. And you got Maryann, the Alligator Girl, he said. A smart-ass. He told me that Showalter's freaks (They call themselves freaks, he said. Nothing wrong with that.) came from every part of the country where people put their not-right children in attics and root cellars and haylofts. There were freaks from Alabama and Mississippi, which you'd expect, he said, but also from New Jersey and Pennsylvania.

Mr. Wilson said, "Western Pennsylvania was a gold mine. We got Legless Louis there and Dimples Delight."

He said that Mr. Showalter still drove up to people's houses, if he heard they had a freak in the family, or he'd be driven by Lucius Wilson himself, who'd pave the way, a Bible in one hand and a contract in his pocket. Sometimes, the parents beg you to take their kid, to give the kid a chance. Sometimes, he said, the kids beg you, so they don't have to live out their days in the cellar. He handed me a flour sack for my things.

The girls' wagon was a tidy navy blue with white scalloped trim around the windows. It looked like a school dress in a catalogue. Mr. Wilson knocked and we waited at the bottom of the stairs. I heard their voices and quick steps to the door. The Alligator Girl let us in. She was in a green terry bathrobe and shorter than me, covered with a thick, bumpy hide, exactly like a pink alligator. The rough, uneven skin ran up most of her face and around her eyes, like a mask. She stood with a book in one hand and when she saw me, she sat back on her bed and began to read, furiously.

Her roommate, the Lobster Girl, was small and pretty with hands fused into large pink claws. She was whitening her shoes like a regular girl. I ducked, not to bang my head getting in the little wagon. I saw two built-in bunks on opposite sides, like pictures I'd seen of ships' quarters, and a folding cot with a green blanket, between them, for me. I stood there, holding my flour sack.

"Well, aren't you Gulliver among the Lilliputians," the Alligator Girl said. "Plus, you have a flour sack."

The Lobster Girl laughed and said, "Jeez, Maryann. She can't help it if she's not a shrimp like us."

Mr. Wilson bowed and walked out, saying, This here is Lorena Hickok, she's working in the front office, so mind your manners.

I had nothing to change into and the two of them watched me sit on the end of the cot. Both of them were deformed and disfigured and probably not even safe out in the wide world, but at Showalter's Étoile du Nord, we faced off as three teenage girls. The other two had real beds and shampoo and toothpaste and they were the right size for this wagon and I was odd man out.

"Do you have nightclothes?" Maryann, the Alligator Girl, said, and I shook my head.

Maryann said, "Nothing I have would fit you."

She held up two small pink nightgowns.

"How about you, Betsy?" she said.

Betsy said, with great kindness, "You can sleep in your underclothes, Lorena. Tomorrow, I'll tell Miss Paula that you could use a few things. There'll be something, there always is."

"I guess," Maryann said. "You're big. I always wanted to have a bit more presence but 'can one desire too much of a good thing?' That's from *As You Like It*."

"Jiminy, Maryann," Betsy said. "Who cares? Sleep tight, Lorena. Dream of handsome men."

She giggled and I thought we could be friends.

I put my clothes and my socks on my cot and stood there in my shabby underwear, in agony.

"We're not modest," Maryann said. "What's the point? I mean, *c'est pour quoi?*"

I said good night. I would have picked up that Maryann was an educated girl, even if she didn't have a leather set of Shakespeare on a shelf over her bed. She saw me looking.

"Do you adore Shakespeare?" she said. I didn't answer right away. I had never used the word *adore* in my life. Maryann sighed and pulled up her blanket.

"Welcome to the wagon, Lorena."

Maryann put out the lamp over her bed and Betsy did the same. I lay in the dark, for a long time, crying into the flat pillow and looking out the window over Betsy's bunk. Men were moving around. I saw the firefly ends of their cigarettes.

In the morning, both girls were gone, beds made, towels hung up.

Mr. Wilson knocked on the wagon door. He picked up a couple of doughnuts for us and said that probably I needed a bigger breakfast but it would have to wait, because he was behind in everything. Miss Paula, the costume manager, had been and gone, leaving behind a pair of patched men's trousers, with a thick belt, a pair of what Mr. Wilson called Turkish slippers (shoes with the satin toes curled up and the sole very thin), and a soft, clean man's shirt. I changed and took dictation in my bare feet, to save my slippers, sitting under an old sign that said *Delight, Entertain, Mystify*, making notes while Mr. Wilson read off the list of who to bribe in Tyndall for tomorrow's show. He handed me a cup of coffee. I wasn't going to Chicago, just yet, or to high school, or to find my kind Aunt Ella. This here was an adventure. A big man with a pointed beard stuck his head in. Mr. Wilson jumped up.

"Mr. Showalter. Sir."

"Gerry heard about the new girl. He has an idea. Send the greenie over there."

I looked up and the big man walked out. Mr. Showalter did not address people like me directly.

Mr. Wilson walked me across the field.

"Hey, Sunshine, I brought a friend. Miss Lorena Hickok."

A wiry, dark-haired man sat outside his wagon, lathering his face in front of a hand mirror and shouting, "'She's gonna shake, she's gonna bake, she's gonna scorch your eyes and then bathe them with her beauty.' How you doing, Lucius? How you doing, kid?"

One of the smaller banners, purple, yellow, red, and blue, with star and moon shapes punched out, and gold fringe along the edges, hung on the side of their wagon and they'd strung fairy lights around the windows and along the roof. A man came out in a flowered silk wrapper and dungarees stuffed into his boots. He was tall and slim. His hair was cut regular style on one side and pinned up like a woman's on the other.

"I'm Gerry," he said. He kissed my hand and said, "Brother and Sister in One Body."

Sunny said, "I'm Sunny Florent. Ballyhoo. Ger, you're not thinking of her for the cooch."

Gerry caught my eye, to say, Stand up straight, and I did, even though I agreed with the other man. I could just see me clumping around on the stage in nothing much while a bunch of men who looked like my father made remarks.

"You never know," Gerry said. "You remember Bertile? Some men like a big girl. She's got nice eyes."

"You're the boss," Sunny said.

Mr. Wilson waved to us and went back to his office, his hair bright in the sun, his suit shining.

"Stay for supper," one of the men said.

. . .

By the time we'd brought plates and bottles and platters to the picnic table, Alligator Girl (Maryann) and Lobster Girl (Betsy) had come over in their linen shifts and felt slippers, with a bunch of wildflowers in a milk bottle for the table. Gerry sat between Betsy and me. I watched to see who was going to help Betsy with the chicken and the dumplings, the size of my fist. I tried not to make a fool of myself, staring at her fused fingers, tight around the fork and knife and sawing away.

"You getting used to us?" Gerry said. He ran a finger up my arm. "Oh, you got the heebie-jeebies?"

He put chicken and potato salad on my plate. I ate my chicken as quietly as I could, trying not to make any big gestures, or knock over my water glass, or demonstrate that I was unfit to be there.

"Here's what you need to know," Gerry said. "Every rube thinks they're better than we are and every freak knows the truth. It's us who are just plain better than them."

"I don't think I'm better than anyone," I said. "Believe me, I don't."

Maryann patted my arm, kindly.

"He doesn't mean you in particular," she said. "He's speaking in general. And, in general, people come to us to be horrified, or amused, or both and, even more, just to feel better. These are poor people scraping by in one-horse towns, hoping for electricity. Like if you're fat with a pretty face, you're mourning your fate, and then God is kind enough to put in front of you a fat girl with a mustache and a port-wine birthmark. We're a comfort, we are. God's conspicuous errors."

"Isn't she something," Betsy said. "Maryann could have gone to college. She could have *taught* college."

"Not too late," Gerry said, and Maryann tossed her head, like she had a headful of curls, instead of what she had, which was a plaid newsie cap on top of her poor, scaly, almost hairless scalp.

Gerry bowed to her.

Betsy said, "We're not deaf, ya know. We hear what they say. Oh mumble mumble, look at her arms. Look at his little titty. They must think once you're onstage, your ears just close up. And we see them too. We see them and I'm telling you, those people, they don't know nothing. The worst of us are still better than rubes."

"Amen," Gerry said. He put down his wineglass and did a little tap dance on the wooden deck.

Gerry said, Lorena and I are taking a walk.

We walked past the edge of the wagons, toward the animals. He held my hand.

"I don't think the cooch is right for you."

"Because I'm plain," I said. "And, I'm too big."

"You need to cut that shit out," he said. "You're not plain. And big's no problem. You got men out there who'd love to bounce on top of you, firm young thing that you are. Lucius Wilson, maybe. Don't you worry."

He kissed me on the cheek. "I never made any money till I took my pants off, sweetheart. I'm not saying you have to go that way."

Every week, we packed up and moved on, from Tyndall, to Plankinton, to Lake Preston and then Tracey, Minnesota, where the rousties added dream catchers with red and blue streamers and Indian headdresses to the decorations. I got up every morning with Maryann and Betsy. The girls folded me into their morning routine. Maryann was the most disfigured and the smartest and the cruelest. With long sleeves and stuffed mittens or gloves on, Betsy could go out in the world. Betsy and I gave Maryann all the privacy we could. Betsy had me brush her hair, which she could do, but not easily, and it gave us both something to pay attention to while Maryann undressed and dressed. Betsy's hair was beautiful, "in the freak show manner," Maryann said.

"You highlight the deformity," she said. She modeled for us, like she was selling gowns at Marshall Field's. She held one hard, pink, completely scaled arm up and traced its pretty curve with her other, equally awful-looking hand. She kept her wrists high and her hands tilted, like a showgirl. She put both hands on her small waist, leaning forward. The only place without scales was the bridge of her nose and her upper lip.

"But you also want to point out the ways in which we are *not* deformed." She squeezed her small waist even tighter and then she pulled Betsy's long braid.

The two of them sat on their bunks to watch me change out of my nightgown, which belonged to the office lady who left, and then get dressed. The watching seemed fair, to all of us. I stood at the foot of my bed and pulled the nightgown over my head. I stood there in just my knickers, looking like who I was, a good-sized girl from South Dakota, who could churn butter and, if I was lucky enough to be somewhere that had a healthy cow, help any farmer deliver a calf. Maryann was looking for flaws but Betsy just cupped her breasts and looked at mine.

"You really do have a very nice chest," she said.

I put on my camisole and tightened the ribbons a little. I knew it was bad manners to rush.

I blushed and put on my shoes while they waited, and the three of us walked out through the wagons, our arms entwined.

. . .

"Everyone's liking you," Gerry said.

I was kneading his shoulders before his rehearsal. He said I had strong hands and he could use the help. He said singing and dancing, as both sexes, made for a goddamn demanding show.

We did tug-of-war with a towel, to loosen him up, then I sat down beside him and helped him pull his knee to his ear. He stood up, shaking out his arms and legs, and told me to stand completely still, or else he'd clip me in the mouth. He swung one long leg up on my shoulder. He dropped his head back and bent his whole torso away from me. Both hands landed on the floor and he rested his right foot on my right shoulder. I could smell the chalk and sweat and a sharp, fruity cologne, from his tights.

"You're good," I said.

"I'm not that good. I'm just more flexible than most men, which is why I am so good at being not half man and half woman, but— all woman and all man."

He sang it out, sonorously, even from the floor, and flipped himself upright, putting a hand on me to get his balance.

"Did you hear Sunny doing my ballyhoo, last night? Sunny's a hot ticket, these days. 'You can only see this extraordinary exhibit if you are over eighteen or under eighty. Under eighteen and you won't understand it, over eighty and you won't be able to stand it!'"

Gerry brought out his radio and stretched his hamstrings on a bale of hay. He found some ragtime.

"I love the Peabody," he said.

He swung me around.

"This was invented by a big fat guy," he said. "That man made the most of what he had, and what he had was more to love. You get me?"

Gerry took me by the hand.

"You be the girl," he said. "We're gonna rumba."

He arched his back and pointed his right leg forward, knees pressed backward, hips high. I stood there, as he must have expected, like an old lady, with a mop. He put two fingers on my shoulder and walked them back and forth. He swung around in front of me and put his other hand on my shoulder blade. He took my hand and put it way around his neck.

"You're around me. And, two-three—four," he said, and pulled me toward him.

I stepped forward and stopped.

"Keep going. Right, rock, left. Right, rock, left."

I shuffled forward and stopped.

He slapped my cheek lightly.

"Don't be a goop," he said. "We're the same height. That's good."

He opened a trunk and brought out a bottle of hooch and two coffee cups.

"What are we celebrating?" I said.

"Nothing. Payday. Your birthday. Any excuse for a little Missouri moonshine."

"It's not my birthday," I said, although I hated to argue with Gerry even that much. We drank our shots of moonshine. I coughed behind my hand.

"All I'm saying is, I think we could look cute together."

"I'm not cute," I said, and I wanted to cry. I wasn't cute. I knew goddamn well I wasn't cute and if Gerry was telling me, to my face, that I was cute, it was because something was making him lie to me. Gerry dragged us through a shim-sham-shimmy routine. I learned the names for the flap, the stamp, the stomp, and the shuffle and I don't think I did a single step right.

"Lookee here. We want you to stay. Miss Paula's cousin's gonna hip-check you off your job when we get to Red Wing. She's a favorite of Mr. Showalter's. I'm trying to find something for you."

"Well, sure as shit, dancing with you ain't it."

I pulled my sweater around me and stomped back to the wagon. Gerry called out, Good night, kiddo, but I knew I'd had a chance and had fallen smack on my big, fat face.

In the morning, I made the flyers for the next town and Mr. Wilson read my press release. That's the stuff, he said. You tell 'em what's what with us. You start with a real ass-grabber and then give 'em the facts. They run it like it's news and ain't we got fun.

Mr. Showalter came in. He watched me type for a moment and looked over at Lucius, who shrugged. Mr. Showalter gave the tiniest shake of the head.

That night, after flyering in four towns, I came back to my wagon. Gerry'd left me a note on the mirror, asking if I could come by and help him stretch.

Gerry and I did the routines, including the one that opened up his chest. I pulled both of his arms behind him and tugged his left hand up to his right shoulder blade and then the right hand.

"It's all about flexibility," he said. "Illusion and flexibility."

He wasn't wearing an undershirt and I could see, as I hadn't before, the soft part of his chest and the hard one. He saw me looking.

"I don't bite," he said. "Neither do they. We are done here, sugar-pie."

He took me back to his wagon, which was a narrow version of mine, with one bed, a faded, patchy quilt, a metal washbasin, and a good mirror bright and clear, with six round lightbulbs around it, strung on a cord. He put four biscuits on a metal plate, with a little pool of honey and bright red berries, frosted in sugar.

"Currants," he said. "They're so sour, your whole mouth'll turn on you, but the sugar makes them sweet and sour. Plus, all those vitamins, we can fight off beriberi."

The biscuit was still warm and filled with bits of bacon. I could have eaten bacon biscuits with Gerry all night.

"It pays to flatter the cook," he said.

He pushed his hair back, and smiled, just a little, with one corner of his mouth turned up, toward his dimple. He looked like a movie star.

"Do you like my smile?" he said.

"It's a nice smile," I said.

"Damn right. Anyone can have a nice smile," he said. "Within reason. Not every freak, obviously, and not some rube with his two front teeth missing, but you, for example, you could smile."

"I don't like to."

He kissed me on the mouth and while I was blinking like a clubbed calf, he held my face in his hands.

"I don't feel like I have so much to smile about," I said, and I was sorry right after I said it.

He took his hands off my face and cracked his knuckles.

"Oh, poor you. I can see what you mean. Here you are, two decent legs, two arms, nice enough pink skin, black curly hair. You can read, write, and type with the parts of the body meant for those activities. You're doing public relations. You got a pair of tits that are really coming along. I see what you mean. You're fucking tragic."

Gerry wasn't having it. Carny people'd punch you in the face before they'd let you tell them your troubles and strangle their own selves before they'd tell you theirs.

He lay down on the bed and patted the space next to him. I lay down, like it was a medical procedure, and he laughed.

"I think you can take off your shoes. God love you," he said when I did. "Who gave you those shoes?"

I'd replaced my Turkish slippers, with small men's wing tips from the lost and found. They were a little big on me, but they were actual shoes, shiny leather with rubber heels and a sturdy sole. Until Gerry looked at them, I'd thought only that they were the best shoes I'd ever owned.

"I'm scared to ask," he said. "How 'bout your socks?"

My socks were plain white cotton and the only thing wrong with them was that I had to wear them three days in a row, because I only had two pair.

"I'm joshing you," he said. "Come on and lie down beside your Uncle Gerry. Or your Aunt Gerry."

He slid the straps of his undershirt down across his shoulders. The right shoulder was muscular and tan. The left was a little softer and whiter. He pulled his undershirt off all the way, rolling it down his body like a tight dress, raising his slim hips to get it off. I sat beside him, trying to see what he was doing, without watching. He pulled the sheet aside and lit another candle. The left side of his chest was shaved smooth, right up to the left side's patch of black hair. His whole torso was honey color and firm, his ribs almost raising ridges under the fine skin.

"See," he said. "You wanna tell me your story, you can do it now."

I didn't want to. I couldn't talk because I was holding my breath. I had no man to compare with Gerry. I'd caught a glimpse of my father once when he was changing his clothes, back before I was scared of him. I saw the pink turkey parts between his legs and thought, That? When the big girls told me about husbands and wives, I'd thought they were making it up, keeping some more terrible truth from me.

His hair down there was dark brown. On one side, he left it tufty and full. He may have even teased it a little, it stuck out so. On the other side, it was a triangle of neat curl, edged like a flower bed. I looked away and he put my hand on the hair.

"It's okay," he said. "Pretty tame."

His penis moved a little under my fingers and I screamed and put both hands between my knees. Gerry laughed. He propped himself up on one elbow and his left breast, the one that was like a girl's, fell forward. It was small, much smaller than mine, and the nipple was darker. I never had much access to mirrors but when I was at the O'Neills', I took advantage of their electric light and their indoor plumbing and their bright bathroom mirror. I studied myself. I wasn't thrilled about what I saw but it wasn't mysterious.

"Nothing to it," he said softly. "Once you know what people expect, you just give it to 'em."

He put my hand on the flat side of his chest.

"This?" he said. He moved my hand to the breast side. "Or this?"

I felt sick. I had never touched a man's bare chest before. I had managed, with some twisting and oh-pardon-me, to at least brush up against Lottie when she was in just her nightie. I rolled on my side. I laid my hand on his chest. I pressed down on the flat plate of muscle, on the tiny nipple, like an acorn tip. I could feel a few wiry hairs under my fingers.

"That's nice," he said. "Nice for me. Nice for you?"

It was not nice, as I understood the word. Touching his girl breast, which was as close as I was ever going to get to an actual girl, made me sweat. It made me want, desperately, to find a girl at the end of the breast. The other side led to what was really there: a man with one soft white shoulder and one thick tan one and only one small, puffy breast and I didn't want to kiss a man, which I had only just now understood. Every woman I'd longed for, I'd understood to be special. Since I was nine, I'd told myself that even though, of course, I hoped for a husband someday, these special women interrupted my trajectory, but only briefly and only because they were so special. Now, I knew that wasn't true. Women were not interruptions, for me.

Gerry said, "Enough about me."

My cami and my knickers were only a little cleaner than my socks. Gerry's gaze was curious and pleasant. I wasn't sure what lust looked like. I tried to imagine how I had looked at Lottie or even, and my face got hot, how I'd felt when Mrs. Miller hugged me. Gerry pulled on a pair of pink silky knickers.

"Let's pretend we're both girls," he said. "I've never been a girl with another girl."

I figured that meant he'd tried all the other possibilities and my head swam.

I lay down and sat up and lay down, like a kid with a fever. Gerry sighed and sat up with me.

"It's okay," he said. "I thought it might go okay. I thought I saw . . . not like this."

"I'm sorry," I said. "I would—it's like you said. I would like to be a girl with another girl."

"And I'm not a girl." He shrugged. "Well, you're right, I'm not. But, hey, let's look at the silver lining—now you know for sure you like girls. So you don't have to marry a man. Y'know, by mistake."

I sat up. Gerry sighed again. He put his arm around my waist and held me still.

"Here's what I'm thinking. We get comfortable with each other and then we try to do a dance number. You do like me, but in reverse. Build up your left side, use my dumbbells, get a suntan. Maybe a half mustache, glued on. We'd keep one side as girly as possible. So then, we could do a tango and trade parts. I'd be the guy, you'd be the girl and then—whammo—other way."

I didn't want to perform. I was no more going to tango than fly and I didn't want to be half boy and half girl. I didn't think I was such a terrible girl that I should just give up being one.

I wanted to cry. I wasn't a true freak. I didn't have a talent or a deformity that people would pay to see. I was a rube and rubes were the worst.

"No tears," Gerry said. "Forget it. We'll just take it easy."

He wrapped his kimono tightly and put his hair back, on both sides.

I lay back down and pretended to sleep. I studied the quilt. Gerry arranged and rearranged us. He spooned me. He rolled me on my side and made me spoon him. He guided my hand down and moved my hand the way he wanted and through it all, I pretended to be asleep and he pretended to think I was asleep. After, I wiped my hand on the underside of the quilt and sat up, rocking in misery. I missed that bacon biscuit and the early part of the evening when I thought dawn was going to come and find me and Gerry still talking and laughing.

Light broke and we heard the rousties taking down the poles and folding up the big canvas. I'd forgotten it was moving day.

Gerry said, "Maybe you don't make the move with us. Maybe you head out. You head east and we head west and never the twain shall meet."

I sat on the bed, tugging at the stitching until it opened and the thin stuffing came out. Gerry slapped my hand.

"Oh no, I'm not having that," he said. "It's time for you to beat it, sugar-pie."

By the time I stood up, he was dressed and waiting for me to put on my shoes.

Gerry walked me back to my wagon. He stuffed my clothes into a small leather valise. He held up three dollars to show me, and put that in a green silk coin purse. He patted me on the shoulder. "I don't want to see your uncoordinated ass still here when the sun comes up. Bus is a mile down the road and coming in one half hour."

I skipped over Gerry entirely, for Eleanor. I said that I'd joined a circus for a few weeks and learned to type. I said that a man had made advances and I rejected them and that I caught the bus away from all that to Chicago for high school and on to Battle Creek and the beginning of Lorena Hickok, Girl Reporter. Eleanor said, as I hoped she would, You're just so interesting.

I told Eleanor what I could. Chicago wasn't terrible. My Aunt Ella was kind. I ran through high school in no time, trying hard to catch up. I overshot and got to college on a scholarship that didn't cover food or clothes, and I did what smart, poor girls do. I cleaned houses. I ate the leftovers off other people's plates and I read other people's textbooks when they left them out on the library tables. I went to any party I could find and I was first at the bar and first to dump a bowl of nuts into my pocket. I slept under my coat. I didn't smell great. The life those college people had, the cashmere sweaters and winter gloves, the lined boots and pert hats, were not for the likes of me and I didn't have the nerve or the discipline to stay.

I went to Battle Creek and got a job at the newspaper, thanking Lucius Wilson for teaching me the who, what, where, and when.

I told Eleanor I got my first bylines, writing about people headed for the Kellogg sanitarium to eat breakfast cereal and get cured of what ailed them. I stayed just long enough to move into an apartment with a nice girl and her cat and I didn't mention the girl or the cat to Eleanor. I kissed the girl and went to Milwaukee, to start my next life.

More, later, Eleanor said.

Longing Is Like the Seed

. . . .

I hustled for the train. Eleanor was already there, waiting for me, sitting very straight in the middle of the seat. She'd kept her hat and gloves on. She looked tired and her face didn't change when she saw me. She sighed.

I said that the Potsdam diner was a delight. She said that after the funeral there was corned beef and cabbage and homemade beer. She said the service was Irish Catholic and heartfelt. I hung up my coat and made a show of taking out my notebook and doing my job, and asking about her husband's ambitions. People said the governor seemed to have a knack for climbing the ladder, regardless of how he'd done on the lower rungs and I repeated that.

"You're very sharp, with your observations," she said.

She looked at me, with those extraordinary eyes, light and clear as a Maine lake, speckled with deeper blue. I didn't mean it, I thought. I don't care. I will praise your husband until my tongue sticks to the roof of my mouth. I will pretend not to know about the actual duties of Missy LeHand. I will see only what you want me to see. Suddenly, she put both hands on my face and I still have no idea what she said about Franklin's ambitions.

We both leaned forward.

"Thank you for listening before," she said. "Thank you for talking."

"I'm not done," I said. "And you can tell me anything. It's off the record."

"Let's have dinner and I'll tell you about the beginning and end of my education," she said.

The steward brought dinner to our compartment: boiled pork on a bed of watery peas and for dessert, two slices of canned pear, faintly green at the edges. I said it sure was Depression Dining. Eleanor said that she approved, that there was no need for frills, that frills would be abhorrent, now, when so many were suffering. I ate my canned pears and thought, Eleanor, you have never eaten food like this in your life, except when you wanted to. We've told our sad stories and what is remarkable is not how alike we are in our dead mothers and tragic pasts, but how different Orphan looks, from your life to mine. I went out for a cigarette and looked out at the dark-blue shapes and deeper shadows racing past. The yellow lights of the train showed more trees, more fields, more track.

I came back to the compartment. The plates were gone and Eleanor had pulled down the shade.

"No one here but us chickens," I said, and thought that if I could just gag myself, this would go so much better.

"My greatest teacher looked a little like you," she said. "She was not as tall as you. She was not . . . willowy. Mademoiselle Souvestre was *planted*. She had the most magnificent head, like a goddess. White wavy hair, always worn back, like you wear yours. Strong brows. Beautiful, fearless eyes. Bright, Prussian blue. You really do look a little like her. I was living with my grandmother, my brother Hall and I, with her and all our glamorous aunts and uncles. I locked my door every night when my poor uncles were on the warpath. And, my Aunt Tissie heard about some of the problems and she must have dropped every aristocratic name she could muster, to get my grandmother to let me go to Allenswood.

You know, all the Strachey girls went to Mademoiselle Souvestre and the Barney girls, and my grandmother gave in. I was fifteen. It was beautiful. It was in Wimbledon Park and it looked just like Somerville College, at Oxford. It was my Oxford."

I barely understood anything she said, except about the wild uncles.

"I bet you were lovely," I said.

"I think most fifteen-year-old girls are," she said.

I didn't argue.

"I have never been so happy in my life," she said. "Ever. I was a favorite. Actually, her supreme favorite. I cannot believe I'm saying that."

I told her I'd been a favorite too and she grinned.

"You know. I got to sit next to her at dinner. Every night. I had wonderful friends too. We all sat together. If you spoke English, a single word, that was a crime and you might have all of your belongings dumped on your bed. But my French was quite good. Still is. My Italian was passable. *Abbastanza buono.* My German, well, *furchtbar.* Terrible. She thought my clothing was dreadful. She did say that. She had a very sharp tongue. She was wonderfully witty but not always kind and she had a real temper, which I thought would terrify me, but it didn't. I had a friend who couldn't stand it, she was scolded so often, and she left. I watched her go from my window, and I felt for her but mostly I thought, How can you bear to leave? It made me work harder, to please Mademoiselle. She could *shred* an essay. She ordered a beautiful red dress for me, burgundy, really, for parties and dances. She ordered it. For *me.* She said I should be proud of my height and dress like a woman, not a baby. Oh, I loved that dress."

Her face lit up and I saw the girl, complete.

"Mademoiselle was fierce, she could strip the paint off the walls. She encouraged ferocity. She had no patience with docility.

See, just like you. And she took us through a classical education, and critical analyses of text, and history, and the languages and literature. If you couldn't make an argument, you had no place there. And there was no shirking and no laziness. She admired effort and ambition. I am carrying on, I'm afraid."

I loved her showing off, tossing around the foreign words, letting me see all the pleasure she took in her once giddy, delighted self. I am done for, I thought.

"She took me all over France, during the holidays, sometimes just me. Oh my goodness, it was such a privilege to travel with her. She knew everything. She believed in beauty, in knowledge, and in social justice. She believed in fighting for what was right, even if you lost, and she believed that her girls had a moral obligation to make the world a better place. Marie Souvestre made me," Eleanor said.

She put her head back against the seat.

"I cried for a month when my grandmother dragged me home for my coming-out party. Mademoiselle argued, I argued, but we lost. We corresponded until she died, two weeks after my wedding. Two weeks after. My wedding gown was pretty but it was nothing to that burgundy dress."

"I would have loved to see you in that dress," I said, and she blushed and I leaned forward and thought, And we're off.

PART TWO

Heart of My Heart

. . . .

Friday afternoon, April 27, 1945
29 Washington Square West
New York, New York

I'm making tuna salad when the phone rings.

"Hello? This is Anna Roosevelt Boettiger, Mrs. Roosevelt's daughter. Is that you, Lorena? What are you doing at the apartment?"

No one else she knows sounds like me. I sound like the hayseed I am and the smoker I was and the drinker that I expect I'll continue to be. Anna asks to speak to her mother and I say she's sleeping and Anna says, Could you check and see if she's awake? When I don't bother putting down the receiver and pretending to walk down the hall to check, her voice tightens.

"Is 'she's sleeping' code for she doesn't want to speak to me?"

It could be code for that. I certainly wouldn't be opposed to using code like that.

"She's actually asleep, Anna," I say.

There's a long pause and if I've been wondering how Anna will ask me, who she despises in the most genial terms, to smooth things over with her mother, who she has betrayed, I don't have to wait long.

"I was worried. I've hardly heard from her since the funeral. That's not like her."

No, it isn't. Eleanor is the one who calls, the one who cares, the one who sits by the sickbed all night. Losing her mother and father and being raised by a bunch of rich crazies, who couldn't find their way out of their own fern-and-statue-stuffed cuckoo's nest, made Eleanor fierce about attachment and control. I wish I'd known her when we were girls. I wish she'd traveled in Europe when she could, with all those glamorous French lesbians and sensible Englishwomen, and studied everything she'd wanted to and not just come home, like a good girl, to meet and marry Franklin, who was nothing special at the time. I wish she hadn't had so many children and lost the one she loved the best. (Some nights, she woke me up, crying for him. Franklin Junior was eleven pounds and the biggest, most beautiful baby in the world, she said. His smile, she said.) I wish she hadn't had to stand by, mute and miserable, while a parade of Sara Delano–trained nannies and Sara Delano herself spoiled and scared the children, undermining my darling at every turn. Franklin said that she was lucky to have a mother-in-law who pitched in.

I know Franklin was fun. The children all remembered when he could walk, playing Hide-and-Seek at Campobello or giving piggyback rides through the Hyde Park woods, and no one knew more about stamps and coins, if you like that. Even for me, his reading and reciting aloud at Christmas was a treat. Once, at a family party (two big Scotches, which is how I usually managed), I recited "Casabianca" ("The boy stood on the burning deck . . .") and Franklin and I did the last stanza together, him roaring in with an English music hall accent. Everyone clapped, in surprise. He gave me a seated bow, and I gave him the same, from my chair that was always too close to the fire but faced Eleanor.

I don't blame Franklin. He wanted what he wanted, when he wanted it, like the rest of us, and children get in the way of that. Even when I got to know them, as grown people, the five of them were still asking for the moon, looking for handouts and praise and treats, every morning. He loved them when they looked good (often) and when they did well (not often) and I don't think he minded when they all fell short, because everybody in the world understood exactly what they were falling short of. The boys watched Franklin, like there was a trick to becoming president and they could master it and get there, but Anna knew that nothing like that was going to happen to a girl. She studied both parents and Franklin was the happier one. She saw him roll his eyes, when her mother came in with a request, an opportunity to help someone. Never mind that he'd sent Eleanor to research the request, to find the opportunity. Never mind that Eleanor made him look good on the left, and gave him wiggle room on the right, his whole political career. (Oh well, that's my missus, he'd say with a wink to some angry cracker in a white suit.)

The only thing that mattered to Anna was being bathed in the sunshine of her father's love and I don't think that made her worse than the rest of them. If her father were Stalin, Anna would have been cheerfully counting up dead Jews and chilling the vodka. Eleanor's love was like some shabby old footstool. Everyone used it without wanting it and no one ever gave it a moment's thought.

"Well, Anna, your mother and I are going through a lot of condolence letters."

I hope that sounds like code for We are balling the jack, little lady.

She sniffs, chilly and disappointed. That sniff is the way she's most like her late grandmother, my least favorite person. I would rather have sat naked in a steam bath with Franklin than had tea with Sara Delano Roosevelt.

"I'm sorry you weren't able to come to my father's funeral," Anna says, and her voice rises a little. She isn't entirely sure I wasn't there. In all the hustle and bustle, the comings and goings of ambassadors and presidents and friends and enemies and more lesbian civil servants than you could shake a stick at, I can hear she's worried that she just didn't see me.

"Well, I was very ill or I would have been there. And I'm here now."

I'm giving up subtlety. It's never done anything for me.

"This is such a difficult time. How does my mother seem to you? I mean, she and Tommie tore through the White House, packing up like nobody's business."

"You know your mother. Give her a list and Tommie's help and she'll conquer the world."

We both laugh. Once, Anna and I snuck in mile-high corned beef sandwiches, and ate them where Eleanor couldn't find us. Anna carried two bottles of Coca-Cola in her bag. I had a tub of potato salad and a flask in my briefcase.

Years ago, when I was a young devil, I was good friends with a girl, a painter, and had hopes of sleeping with her honey. The honey had come to my place out of sorts and looking for a good time. She prepared for the good time, drinking three shots in a row and slamming them down the way amateurs do. She passed out on my bedroom floor. I called my friend and she came over. We stood over the passed-out girl, two women of the world (as we thought then) and, as mad as she was at me, and as ashamed of myself as I was, we shared a beer and laughed.

Every once in a while, there was that kind of laugh, between Anna and me.

. . .

"Oh, Hick. Did my mother tell you about . . . Warm Springs?"

Her mother had. Her mother had called me as soon as she got back from the Little White House in Warm Springs.

Eleanor said to me, "My daughter brought Lucy Mercer all the way to Georgia to be with Franklin. She says she didn't but I know she did."

She coughed, instead of crying. "I could never betray anyone, in that manner," she said.

And it was true, she never could. I could. I had. Franklin could have and had done, probably five times before breakfast, most days of the week.

I told Eleanor that I knew that, and loved her for it. She'd already told me every awful minute she had in Warm Springs, getting Franklin's body back to Washington, and every awful minute after that. Warm Springs was Franklin's great comfort and his best self. He'd tried every reasonable and ridiculous treatment on earth and when he knew he'd never walk again, he tried bathing in the waters that flowed down from Georgia's Pine Mountain and he moved his right leg a few inches. Being one of the world's great con men didn't keep him from falling for the idea of therapeutic waters. He bought that run-down resort in Bullochville, Georgia, for two hundred thousand dollars (Eleanor was horrified, she said, and she had no way to talk him out of it; they were his legs, she said, and he believed), put in a decent pool in 1926, and made it Warm Springs and if no one ever made a recovery from the Pine Mountain water, no one ever got worse from it. He gave hundreds of polio victims the chance to be treated, the chance to be seen as people (some of them were delivered by desperate families, lying on a blanket in the back of a pickup, and some came, bundled into a boxcar, with just the clothes they wore and a pair of crutches) and to get as much help as they could use. Eleanor said that she loved that he loved it, but it was his place, not hers, his cottage, and she was happy to have Missy sleeping across the hall from Franklin and sitting across from him at the dinner table, down there. He was every patient's father, and their friend, and their tireless fundraiser. He was the crippled king and when he told me that he'd rather spend the evening eating canned ham and baked beans with two fourteen-year-old boys from Biloxi, showing him the wheelchair song-and-dance routine they'd worked up, instead of having cocktails with Claudette Colbert, I believed him. He was their Eleanor.

In the last week of his life, he was too tired to visit the patients. Lucy Mercer played hostess. Her friend Elizabeth Shoumatoff painted his portrait. The Secret Service made their rounds and the crazy Roosevelt cousins jockeyed for position at the dinner table. Shoumatoff's turpentine and Lucy Mercer Rutherfurd's thick perfume were still in the air when Eleanor got down there. She sat with Franklin's body.

"I looked at him. I sat alone with him for a few minutes. I kissed him," she said. "How could they think I wouldn't know? Do they think I'm a fool? I had to ride in the car with Cousin Daisy, who *is* a fool. And Cousin Polly."

"Cousin Polly is a crazy, purple-haired bitch," I said. "She should have stayed home with all of her stupid dogs."

"Oh no, she wasn't going to miss a chance to cozy up to Franklin. And she got to tell me that not only was Lucy Mercer cuddling with Franklin in Warm Springs but it wasn't the first time and 'Oh dear, was she letting the cat out of the bag, but Anna knew all about the whole Lucy thing.'"

"That bitch," I said. "Please stay away from her or at least, please don't be so nice to her."

"Lucy Mercer came to the White House," she said. "And everyone knew. Except me. And you."

This was technically true. I'd heard some things but people didn't tell me what they didn't want Eleanor to hear.

"Anna wants to apologize," Eleanor said. "I know I have to let her and I know I have to forgive her but I don't want to do it now. I don't think I can control myself."

"Leave it alone," I said. "You got years."

"Hick?" Anna says.

"Yeah, Warm Springs. That must have been tricky, when your mother arrived."

Anna is not daunted by the likes of me. "It was innocent—"

"If it was innocent, you probably should have told your mother, and then she would have agreed that it was innocent and then on the day of her husband's funeral, your mother wouldn't have had to postpone her mourning, to sit with you while you explained how difficult it was for poor *you*, all that distressing back-and-forth, so your father could have private time, relaxing time, as you keep saying—with Lucy Mercer, that little buffet of relaxation. And not just in Warm Springs, with no one to watch except the staff and the cousins and forty patients with polio traipsing in and out of the Little White House, but even in the real White House and at your mother's dinner table, in the family dining room, in front of people who'd been serving your mother, the First Lady, for twelve years."

"I told my mother. I told her right away, I didn't know about Warm Springs."

"You're full of shit," I say, cheerfully. I do like a fight. "You chose your father over your mother and now you pretend you did it out of love. You did it to cement your position and to give your mother just one more shove to the side. Oh, you kids. You'd run your mother over to get a smile from the old man. And now, who you got? Your mother. And me."

I can hear Anna breathing. If Eleanor were awake, she'd kill me.

"Your mother'll forgive you," I say. "You know she will. That's the whole story, right? She'll forgive you for betraying her. Jesus H. Christ, she'd forgive you for much worse than that, and your father would never, ever have forgiven you for not helping him romance the past, with a little help from Lucy Fucking Mercer."

"Oh, Hick," she says. "All right."

Turning fifty seems to have flattened my moral high ground, like a great left hook. And I do like Anna. She has always been a fool for love, and I like that in a person.

When she was getting divorced and carrying on with John Boettiger, the four of us were a road show for romance, even if the two of them didn't know it. She was in love, John was in love, I was in love, and Eleanor was in love with me. Eleanor was always happy to help other lovebirds. If Al Capone had broken into the White House with a hot dame, Eleanor would have hustled them up to the third floor to give them a little privacy. We were all four of us aglow in 1933. Anna bounced on her mother's bed like a kid, crying and laughing about her great, amorous adventure and Eleanor and I pressed hands where she couldn't see. We touched under tablecloths, beneath napkins, behind the newspaper. When the halls were quiet and the maids had gone, Eleanor unlocked her bedroom door for me and I ran in.

• • •

"It'll be all right," I say to Anna. "Your mother just needs a few days. Tell your brothers to take care of themselves. Maybe they can manage not to steal anything or lie to anyone or knock anybody up, just for a year or two. And you take care of yourself and the babies, and John. It'll be fine."

"Hick," she says, and I think maybe she'll apologize for the sneers and the looks and the careful arrangement of the seating at parties and the gifts that were calibrated to be exactly, or a little less than, what was given to housekeeping and my chest tightens. And I have to laugh at my inner hired girl, always looking for a soft moment with The Family. Anna is no more going to apologize to me than Lucy Mercer is going to apologize to Eleanor for sleeping with her husband and betraying their friendship.

Oh, these pretty, wifey women. I'd read Lucy's condolence note. I took it out of Eleanor's hand to read it and then burn it. Lucy Mercer Rutherfurd sent love and deep sympathy on the occasion of Franklin's death. She wrote that Eleanor was the most blessed and privileged of women and made it clear that she knew exactly what the blessings were. Lucy Mercer Rutherfurd had failed to break up their marriage when they were all young and healthy and she failed again when she was a pretty widow. She showed up for dinner and tea and rides with Franklin in the countryside and still, she herself would wind up nothing more than a racy footnote and Eleanor would always be a front-page story in this country. I should know better than to let Anna rile me.

"Here's one for the books. Your mother sent Lucy one of Shoumatoff's little watercolors of your father. And she did it after she got that smug, cruel, unbearable little note. Your mother is extraordinary."

"I know," Anna says in her small bird voice.

"You don't," I say, and I hang up the phone.

I pull the blanket up over Eleanor. I make a pot of Chinese tea and pour two jiggers of gin into it. In Milwaukee, we used to call it Mother's Ruin but Eleanor wouldn't find that funny. All I care about is getting a little gin inside her so she can rest.

She grabs my wrist. Her hair's half-down and she's struggling to wake up, to get from the last grief to the next.

"Oh, darling, I keep dreaming about those circus people, when you were a girl. I'm glad you got away."

"They weren't *keeping* me," I say. The prissy Eleanor is not my favorite. "And they weren't bad."

She says that she can't bear to think of the bad times I've had.

I don't say anything. I don't say, the two worst days of my life so far have been when my father raped me and that day in the White House, ten years ago, when I waited for you from morning till night, while everybody watched. I waited so long I ran into Franklin twice and got scalded by his grinning sympathy. ("Still waiting for Babs?" he said. "She's somewhere." And he wheeled off to bed.) I'd been expecting her since breakfast. I fixed myself up. I got my skirt and jacket pressed, always walking that thin line between too much effort, which leads to a Minneapolis matron look or else the Oscar Wilde of South Dakota—and no effort at all, which is trousers and a sagging sweater, like an old sailor. Eleanor didn't come home until after midnight. I'd gone to bed. She pushed a scented note under my door and I smelled it, before I saw it. I opened the envelope before dawn and I can still quote the whole goddamn thing. *Je t'aime* and *je t'adore* and I know you have no wish to make me unhappy. It said that the real task for the two of us was to learn how to love and let go and yet keep loving.

When I read that I thought, I am almost fifty years old and the rest of my life will be love and loss, and when I look down the road, I see a fat old woman and her dog, is what I see.

Eleanor reaches for her blouse and fumbles with the pearl fleur-de-lis pin on the collar. She takes the pin off, with her eyes closed, and puts it in my hand.

"He gave it to me. I'm giving it to you."

Another heirloom, from him to her to me.

She lies down again.

"I'm asleep already, dearest," she says. "Wake me on Monday."

I can wait, I think.

Swinging on a Star

....

It's hard to believe that the first thing she says to me, over the cheese and crackers and sidecars, is "Dearest, Tommie will be here bright and early Monday morning. Early."

"I won't linger," I say.

"You're insulted," she says.

Damn right.

"Half and half," I say and I get a kiss for that and I'm more insulted by the reward, like I've mastered Sit and Shake Hands.

"I could stay on," I say, just to see.

Eleanor says, "That would be hard on Tommie, wouldn't it?"

Tommie Thompson's been with the Roosevelts since before me. She lives to serve Eleanor. She'd watch me get hit by a car, and grieve only for Eleanor's distress and my guess is, she feels that way about everyone in the world, including her first husband and her current beau. If Tommie comes in to find me drinking coffee in my pajamas, she'll nod and cough. I'll get a half smile. She'll pace around the living room like it's a boxing ring. Hat on, hat off. Finally, she'll plant herself at the dining room table, pull her hatpin out like she's ready to kill Hitler, take her hat off one last time, open her portable typewriter and say, Mrs. R., let's get started. Then she'll go to the kitchen and make coffee that could strip paint (a cup for each of them) and sit there, square as a house (I should talk) while she waits for me to gather up my things, hang up my towel, and go back to Long Island.

For years, Tommie and I would find ourselves going to the same meetings, jammed in Franklin's elevator. It was a tight fit. We faced each other, there was no other way. We were square women, standing wide front to wide front, smelling each other's morning coffee and cigarettes.

"Goin' up," she usually said. "Ladies' shoes, linens, kitchenwares."

"Secrets of the White House," I'd say and she'd snort.

I walk into the kitchen, which gave me such pleasure to clean a little while ago, and I look for things to break. I don't think Tommie minds me that much. I'm not disloyal, like some. I'm not a snob like the bluestockings, who make anyone who can't quote Sappho and Catullus feel like a shmuck. (I told them Franklin's joke about the sailor and the kangaroo and changed the sailor to Sappho. No one laughed.) I've put a bottle of Scotch under the tree for Tommie every year, and she's done the same for me.

Me and Hick, we're Mrs. R.'s right hands, she'd say to reporters, to Franklin, who grinned and bit his tongue, to the relentless Roosevelt cousins, always sniffing for gossip and gold.

"I certainly don't want to upset Tommie," I call out.

Eleanor doesn't say anything and I walk back to the living room. Only the small lamp is on. She's lying on the couch in her kimono, with her hair unpinned and her eyes closed.

"Sometimes, I get sick of my own self," she says.

"Likewise," I say. "It doesn't matter."

She says, "The first time Franklin was elected president, when he beat the pants off Mr. Hoover, I cried so hard, I couldn't even greet our guests the next morning. We'd just met. I was wild about you. I'd never met anyone like you and I thought, He'll lose and he'll be governor for a while longer and who cares what the governor's wife does anyway. I thought, I'll keep teaching and you and I will be together, all the time. And then he won and I thought, It's over."

"It wasn't," I say.

I covered Herbert Hoover when he entered the White House, saying, "We shall soon, with the help of God, be in sight of the day when poverty shall be banished from this nation." And a year later, stockbrokers were jumping out of windows and farmers were killing their families and hanging themselves from oak trees.

The Crash pushed on, deeper and harder, and Hoover made a few gestures, like an old lady facing the incoming tide. When seventeen thousand World War I veterans gathered on the National Mall to cash in their service certificates, I covered the story. They brought their wives and children. They built tar-paper shacks Hoover could see from the White House. The attorney general ordered the veterans driven out and I covered the story when they resisted. I covered it when American police officers opened fire on decorated veterans of the United States Army and two veterans died of gunshot wounds. I covered the story when Hoover ordered that buffoon Douglas MacArthur to lead the infantry and six tanks to drive out soldiers who had served their country and needed the money they'd been promised. I covered it when the United States Army burned the tar-paper shacks and the veterans left, with their wives and children, leaving behind jackets and diapers, cots, pots and pans. The fires stank to high heaven and when they turned the tanks on the fleeing veterans, I thought, Hide, you cowardly, tightfisted son of a bitch, Roosevelt is coming.

We were on the story of the Depression every day, most of us doing our best to record the lives and deaths of people and shame President Hoover. We called old newspapers "Hoover blankets" and delivered piles of them to the edge of hobo camps. People hitched their broken-down cars and pickup trucks to mules—if they had mules—and Midwestern newpapers ran the photos, calling them "Hoover wagons." Hoover made one cautious mistake after another while people lost their jobs and banks failed, every day. A thousand economists wrote to him, basically saying, Don't be a jackass, and Hoover said, The marketplace will sort it out. It sorted him right out of office. Franklin came in on a tidal wave of decency and great speeches. *(True individual freedom cannot exist without economic security and independence. People who are hungry and out of a job are the stuff of which dictatorships are made.)* The country had a leader. Hired girls had a hero.

We've both showered and washed our hair with French shampoo from before the war. We're sitting on the couch in our old terry robes.

I say, "We look like a pair of polar bears."

Eleanor says, "I have never stopped loving you. That's what I was trying to say."

"I know," I say. "Likewise. You know what I've always loved about you?"

"No," she says, as if she can't recall.

"I always loved when you'd walk into one of Franklin's late-night soirées, with Princess Martha tossing her curls at him like she was on the piano at the Norwegian Box Top, and you'd just clear your throat. That's all you had to do. And they all froze."

She clears her throat to make me laugh.

"I loved that. I did. They just stopped on a dime. You'd pocket their balls and walk out. I loved that, every time."

"Did I seem like a nag?"

I wouldn't call it nagging. It was like having the Statue of Liberty watch you have one beer too many. Everyone except Franklin would shrink a little and Eleanor would purse her lips, as if she was so clobbered with disgust, she couldn't hide it. When I wasn't the victim, I loved it. And when I was the object of her love, when her eyes lit up across the room, when she touched her fingertips to the pulse at the base of her throat, to mark the spot for me, to mark herself, I thought that there was no sacrifice I wouldn't make.

Eleanor leans forward and the strap tears off from her slip and we both hear it.

"That slip's done," I say. "I'm glad."

She pulls it off and I unbutton my shirt. I let my robe open and our tired white flesh meets and what may not look beautiful does feel beautiful.

Eleanor says that we should turn out the light and I say, I will pay you a million dollars to let me look at you.

Every woman's body is an intimate landscape. The hills, the valleys, the narrow ledges, the riverbanks, the sudden eruptions of soft or crinkling hair. Here are the plains, the fine dry slopes. Here are the woods, here is the smooth path to the only door I wish to walk through. Eleanor's body is the landscape of my true home.

The Words the Happy Say

. . . .

SATURDAY EARLY MORNING, APRIL 28, 1945
29 Washington Square West
New York, New York

I wake up before dawn and Eleanor's in the living room, glasses on, tea steeping.

She smiles up at me.

"More letters. Missy's nieces. And her brother too."

"I liked Missy," I say. "I never felt so sorry for anyone in my life."

"I know. Poor Missy. Good heavens, Princess Martha as a rival. Missy deserved better."

We both roll our eyes and Eleanor pushes back an imaginary hat with two fingers and wrinkles her nose at the same time, making her a perfect naughty rabbit, or, if you knew her, a perfect Princess Martha of Norway, Franklin's frequent guest.

"You were very good to Missy," Eleanor says.

I was.

Four years ago, it was warm but not yet hot and Eleanor was traveling for weeks. I was rabble-rousing for Democrats and Missy was in charge of the White House staff party. She wore a nice black crêpe dress, with a lace collar and only a little pink lipstick. Like Eleanor, she was a study in beautiful gray and white and unlike Eleanor, her dress clung, top and bottom. Eleanor always arranged for corsages for the female staff and Missy's was just like Eleanor's, a cascade of three white orchids. I always thought she looked enough like Eleanor to be a younger sister, with better teeth and a stronger jawline, but no one else in the world seemed to have noticed, so I didn't say.

Franklin rolled into the party, wearing a chef's hat and apron, and everyone clapped. He turned on the twinkle and served up a few plates. He winked at Missy, patted me on the arm (Missy's done it up, he said; too bad the missus couldn't come), and wheeled out. Missy called for three busty girls to get up and do their version of the Andrews Sisters and I said to Grace Tully, If I hear "Bei Mir Bist Du Schön" sung one more time by girls who wouldn't kiss a Jewish boy if his life depended on it—and Tully, Franklin's junior secretary, shushed me. Missy put a finger to her lips to scold me and then she clapped both hands to her forehead. She grabbed at the buffet table and brought the tablecloth, the plates, the petits fours tower, and the bowls of fruit down around her.

Oh, she kept saying, oh God. Oh God have mercy, what is this, she said. Her lips turned blue.

Tully grabbed her by the belt going down and I knelt down to catch her. In twenty years, Missy sometimes had a few too many drinks, which was mostly her wish to keep up with the boss, and also, and I have no high ground here at all, her wish to periodically forget that he was the whole world for her and she was a delightful little village for him. I thought this might be only that.

The lead singer caught my eye and signaled the other two. They paused and everyone looked around to see why. The blond singer sat down on a pink velvet ballroom chair. Mabel from housekeeping picked up the fruit and the smashed chocolates, frowning at the waste and at poor Missy, shaking in my arms, peeing on my skirt.

I carried Missy out of the room. Tully followed with Missy's handbag. Two of the Secret Service guys met me at the elevator. We took the elevator to the third floor. I'd never been to Missy LeHand's room before. It was like a maid's room in Hyde Park. One high, joyless window. One narrow twin bed, too short for anyone who'd had a decent childhood. A stained marble basin in a wood vanity so old the lacquer was coming off in dismal brown strips, like the last leaves. There was a big crystal vase filled with fading tulips and some letters weighed down with two snow globes of the White House.

By the time we'd undressed her and put her in her white pajamas, with the pink piping, which were a gift from Eleanor the year before, the doctor was knocking on the door. Her mouth hung open and her right eye fluttered like a moth. The doctor looked at my wet skirt and shoved us out of the little room. I'm guessing it's a heart attack, he said.

Tully and I walked down the hall, Tully still holding Missy's silver jacket. I could slip a note under Franklin's door and he might love me for it. I wrote the note and I stopped outside his closed office door and put it in my pocket. Whoever's job that was, it wasn't mine.

Eleanor came back the next day and bustled while Missy lay there. She was her worst and her best self. She hired a cadre of nurses. She let people know that it was possible that this was all psychological. She arranged for massage therapists and doctors. And when Missy had another, bigger stroke, there was fresh fruit every day, cut very small, which Missy could hardly eat because her left side, from her eye to her chin, wasn't working at all. We had one ceremonial, excruciating visit from Franklin, rolling in with the big laugh and the flowers that Eleanor had put on his lap in the elevator. Eleanor hovered and I walked down the stairs, so as to not kill anyone.

"He hates illness," Eleanor said to me. "It's painful for him to see her this way. Missy is . . . she's always been so lively. And charming."

That's what we all said about Missy. We said it to White House staff. We said it to visitors. We said it to reporters. The idea that Franklin preferred his secretary to his wife didn't offend any newsmen, not the Catholic ones and not the married ones. Eleanor was a Great Lady and what man in Christ's name wanted to be married to that?

At six, every day, Tully came by with carefully sifted news for Missy, which was worse than no news. It was the news that Eleanor and Franklin allowed Tully to give out to the cousins, tidbits designed to look like the real thing. Missy LeHand had been Franklin Roosevelt's confidante and secretary and stage manager and mistress. Her ass had rested on the arm of Franklin's chair, the fabric of her dress flowing over his sleeve, both of them feeling an invisible, electric wire between them. She'd sat in his lap while he looked at top-secret documents or read the paper, with her head on his shoulder. She'd rested her hands on his shoulders while he mused about exactly what lie he would roll out in the middle of lunch with an irate cabinet member and she laughed and gave him a kiss on the temple. Oh, F.D., she said, aren't you a one. She put on the Irish, which he loved; there was no kind of mockery he didn't love. And Franklin would say, when he felt too pressed, or backed into a corner or reminded of something he'd promised to someone in need, who was now revealed to be a colossal pain in the ass, Humankind cannot bear very much reality. We all knew that he'd heard that line from Winston Churchill, who learned it from Clementine Churchill, who had actually read T. S. Eliot's poems.

Eleanor did better than Franklin. She brought embroidered pillows. She had Missy's robe cleaned and bought her two new ones. Cotton, not satin, because it was summer and because there was no point pretending Missy wasn't spilling things down the front. Eleanor came into the room one morning, carrying small green crown-shaped bottles of Inauguration, the perfume Prince Matchabelli (an actual prince) had made for her. It smelled like carnations and burning rubber and we all hated it. Eleanor gave out bottles to every woman she knew. Amelia Earhart sniffed it, twisted the top tightly, and handed it to her husband, George, who put it in his pocket. Eleanor gave a bottle to Tommie, over breakfast. Tommie held it up to the light, admired the green ribbed glass and pushed it back as if it was just too grand for the likes of her. Every time Eleanor put a bottle on my dresser, I put it back in her underwear drawer. She had twenty-five bottles of the stuff.

"Enough for everyone," she said, and she put two of the bottles down on Missy's breakfast tray. "Dear Missy, I am so sorry to run off. Hick, darling, I'm so glad you can visit for a little while with Missy."

Missy looked at me.

"I brought you some things," I said. "We're not going to sit here like dopes. I got cards, I got the newspaper, and I got you this."

I took out the alphabet board I'd found at a school for the deaf.

"Look at this thing." I tapped a few keys encouragingly, as if we weren't both damn good typists.

She took the board in her left hand, which was weak but not useless like the right.

GO.

"I can't go," I said. "You heard her. I'm visiting with you for a little while."

She closed her eyes. I didn't blame her.

I offered Missy bourbon, from the bottle in my bag.

"I won't tell, if you won't," I said. "Just two scholarship girls, grabbing a drink, while the fancy folks go about their business."

She looked right at me, her wide white face trembling.

"I know," I said. "I do know how it is. And you had it much better than I ever did. You weren't cropped out of all the photos. No one in the White House pretended not to know your name. Jesus Christ, Missy, I've come in more back doors and down more hidden staircases, with more fake names than a Russian spy but, you, the attractive secretary and the dashing Great Man, especially dashing while in a wheelchair, everyone loved that story."

Missy and Franklin put a smile on reporters' faces. Eleanor and I were no one's favorite secret. I tended to scowl. Eleanor sometimes turned her face away. We were puzzling. I was not the travel companion the press wanted for her (*Time* magazine said I was rotund, with baggy clothes and a peremptory manner, and no one in the White House said, Oh, my dear, how could they?) and it was clear, to all those men, covering her all the time, that there was something wrong with the picture and the descriptions of me were even worse than the pictures. I'd spent my whole adult life with good-looking women sitting on my knee and expressing interest but in the world of *Time* magazine and *The New York Times,* I was a musical comedy nanny. I was a fat sheepdog in rumpled clothes. (Did they know Eleanor had my suits made? That I was wearing French silk panties, bought and paid for by the First Lady?) My job, as the world saw it, was getting Eleanor Roosevelt from event to event, nipping at Mrs. Roosevelt's heels.

But that was old news and I was still around. I was still having lunch with Eleanor, still finding boxes of hand-me-down evening gowns in my armoire, still getting occasional checks with emphatically kind notes and carrying on with Marion, which made me feel alive. Missy had nothing but bouquets bought by Eleanor.

"Just you and me, kid," I said. "Come on, I'll tell you a story."

Everything I'd seen, she'd seen, except the stories that were too private. I didn't expect her to tell me how it felt, helping Franklin from the chair to the bed and leaving that bed to run up to the third floor at three A.M. She didn't expect me to tell her about the time Eleanor and I found ourselves in ridiculous, middle-aged passion in a not very large dressing room of Bergdorf Goodman, while Eleanor was still First Lady and looking for a new blouse. We were down to our slips and hose, her sitting on my lap, both of us bracing against the collapse of the little chair. It still made me smile.

"I'll tell you what really happened when we went to Yosemite. Everyone loved that disaster."

Her eyes came back to me and her lips lifted a little, on the left side.

Everyone in America knew about our Yosemite vacation, what we privately called "our second honeymoon," because I fell off a horse. Every newspaper covered the story but no one had a photograph and that was luck enough for me. The papers gave a whole column of comedy to Mrs. Roosevelt's bulky sidekick, sliding off a stubborn horse in one of our great national treasures, and into a creek, surrounded by handsome park rangers. I was humiliated but I wasn't hurt and I managed to laugh, for Eleanor's sake.

Oh, Missy, I said. I was just a fool, in public and private on that holiday. I fell off a horse. I told the tourists to go to hell. I don't have your grace, I said.

Who doesn't like to hear that?

Missy nodded.

Once we were back in the lodge, Eleanor hung up my clothes to dry and stuffed my boots with paper and put them by the fire. She poured sherry into two small tin cups and pulled me down to the quilt. It's still just us, she said. We're just Jane and Janet Doe making our way through the Wild West and naturally, mistakes will occur. The fire flickered across her face and she rubbed my sore feet, my aching legs. She swaddled me and kissed my forehead, like I was an invalid, and when the sun came up and there were more horses to ride and more tourists to charm, I smiled like a Roosevelt. I was a good sport and she was very kind, and I appreciated her kindness and she appreciated my good cheer, and somehow, that was that.

In four years, we'd run out of possibilities. She wouldn't leave Franklin until he was out of office, and I didn't actually want her to. When she said she could, I pointed out how important he was to her own goals and to the country. When I said that maybe, we could take a month in New Mexico, maybe we could get our own place in Manhattan, she pointed out that we'd have reporters everywhere, and always would. I couldn't pose successfully as her aide-de-camp because in public, she would take my hand, sometimes, or press up against me, and in spite of myself, I had to tell her not to.

"I am this way with all of my friends," she said. It was true. They were all an endless daisy chain of pats and squeezes, of affection and endearments.

"It looks different when it's us," I said. "I like it. Jesus, Eleanor, I love it, and that's the problem. We do not look like the dearest of friends. Trust me."

"I wonder if we aren't, really, the dearest of friends. Deep down."

. . .

I drove back East by myself. I banged the living daylights out of an old girlfriend in San Fran, pardon my French, and I did my best to move forward without complaint. I didn't succeed, but I did try.

(It became a very popular story back East. For the next year, Franklin and his sons, and every other man in the White House, would give me a poke or a look, whenever the subject of the national parks or horseback riding or even just vacations came up.)

CANT LIVE, Missy wrote. PLS.

"You can," I said. "Looky here."

I took mint and sugar out of my bag. I made us mint juleps in honor of there being some horse race somewhere. I crushed the mint with my fingers and poured her drink into a cup and put in a straw. It was hard for her to get her lips around the straw and she began to cry, only her right eye leaking tears.

Don't worry, I said. I poured the julep into a bowl and I fed it to her.

Missy swallowed a few times and put her left hand up to her mouth, to stop me.

F.D., she typed.

I started to say that I was sure he'd come by soon and I closed my mouth. I was no better than the rest of them.

I packed up my julep fixings. I washed out the bowl. I left the little keyboard on the nightstand. I said that she must know how much all of the Roosevelts loved her and that all we wanted, him especially, was for her to get well.

Franklin had changed his will and let everyone in the family know that if he died before Missy, half of his estate would be put aside for her medical bills and ongoing care. Everyone acted as if this made sense, as if any man would do this for his devoted secretary and announce it to all, and Eleanor kept on with the fruit and the flowers and the visits and so did I. I thought that if I was in Missy's shoes, I would hope somebody'd kill me, and if they couldn't do that, I'd hope they'd visit me and bring the bourbon.

There wasn't enough bourbon.

In February, Missy choked herself with a chicken bone from lunch and if the nurse hadn't come back in to get the sweater she'd left behind, Missy would have died, vomiting blood on her sheets. In March, she set herself on fire in the middle of the night, matchbooks flaming at the four corners of the bed. Her hands and chest were burned. She needed gauze bandages on both hands, for a little while, and a nurse had to feed her and turn pages for her. Come spring, Princess Martha of Norway fled the Nazis and became the White House's effervescent guest. In early May, Franklin came into Missy's room for ten minutes. He went back downstairs to dinner with the princess. Missy had a relapse of some kind and by ten P.M., a nurse and a maid had packed up what Missy had and put her in a car for her sister's house in Somerville, Massachusetts. She could recover there, is what everyone said, by which we all meant, suffer in private and not burn down the White House.

According to the letters from her sister, things got better in Somerville. After eight months, Missy could write her own brief notes, and she did. She didn't write to me but she wrote to Grace Tully, and to Franklin and to Eleanor, both of whom read her short, shaky letters aloud to each other, and sighed. She was walking now, she wrote. She was doing so well, her bed had been moved back upstairs.

Work took me near Somerville and I wrote that I could come

by in a week, with a note from Franklin and gifts from everyone. It was Tommie who put together the package and Tully who ran down to give me a note from Franklin. Anna LeHand Rochon called me at the hotel and said that they would be happy to have me over for tea at 101 Orchard Street.

There was nothing wrong with the house, pictures of Ireland, of the saint with the snakes, of the Irish grandparents, of her late parents, holding their two daughters on their lap, while the oldest, Missy's brother, Daniel, stood aside, his hand on his mother's shoulder. Missy's nieces, whose names I'd learned and forgotten a dozen times, came downstairs, out of curiosity. I stood in the doorway, with my coat and hat still on, next to Missy's sister and the nieces, and we all watched Missy, in a loose sweater and dowdy plaid skirt, walk down the stairs, very slowly. She gripped both stair rails and she came down the way I sometimes do myself, letting one leg do most of the work, always taking the step down at an angle.

I clasped both of Missy's thin hands so as not to knock her over and we walked side by side to the sofa. Finally, one of the nieces took my coat and hat.

I looked behind Missy and saw the big sterling cup Franklin had sent her, with a curly monogram of *MLeH* on it. It had fresh roses in it.

"The Roosevelts have been so wonderful," Anna said. "They send gifts all the time."

Missy nodded and looked toward the coffee table where there was a copy of *The True Story of Fala*, an insipid book about Franklin's dog, written by Cousin Daisy. It was open to an inscription from Franklin, and I picked it up and looked, as I was supposed to.

"You know who's always here?" Missy's sister patted my arm. "Bill Bullitt. He sends notes, he comes by. He sends the craziest gifts, doesn't he, Missy? So extravagant. He's still in love with you, honey."

Missy nodded again.

Most of us thought Bullitt chased Missy to catch Franklin, and no one thought much of him. Before her stroke, she'd carry on stagy, flirtatious phone conversations with him and then hang up, rolling her eyes at whoever was nearby. And last year, when Franklin was completely fed up with the man, he told Bullitt that there'd be no promotions, no cabinet position coming, ever, and he encouraged him to run for mayor of Philadelphia. Bullitt said, All right, he would. And then Franklin called up every captain and cog in the Philadelphia machine the summer of '43 and told them, "Cut his throat." Eleanor told me she'd sat on the couch while he made the calls. He was in great spirits, she said.

Bill Bullitt was an opportunistic, anti-Semitic, Commie-chasing piece of shit. I didn't say that either.

I said, "You look wonderful. Tell me what you've been up to."

Her sister stiffened.

Missy clasped her hands in front of her and rolled back her shoulders. She said, I think: Not much.

Her sister laughed, like Missy was such a comedian. "Oh, Missy, that's not true. You exercise. You read. You're wonderful with Babe and Barbara, those are my daughters. We go to the movies. The President gets us tickets, you know."

"That reminds me," I said. I handed Missy the note from Franklin. She dropped it and picked it up before I could help. She pressed it to her chest and made an ugly little sound in her throat.

Her sister made a move to take it from her and Missy moved it up to her bare skin.

Missy said: F.D.

Anna poured more tea.

Missy said: Loves me.

She nodded. I nodded back.

Anna said that maybe Missy'd like to read it later. Missy nodded, her head tilting left, and then she held the note to her cheek.

Anna said, "It's so wonderful that he took the time to write, honey."

Missy lowered her eyes.

"Speaking of the White House," I said. "Your old beau, Bill Bullitt? Gosh, did you ever hear about the beautiful ball he gave in Moscow, in the thirties? Talk about extravagant."

I gave that story everything I had. I gave them detail upon detail and what I didn't know, I made up. I told them about dancers from the Bolshoi twirling *en pointe* through birch trees placed in the chandelier room, re-creating the Russian countryside. I described the long dining room table, covered with Finnish tulips from end to end, and chicory planted in rolls of wet felt, to make a living lawn, inside the ballroom. There were parakeets and a few pheasants and zebra finches. Zebra finches are so beautiful, I said, and I described them like an avid bird-watcher. Plus, I said, the man brought in goats.

"Goats," Anna said, gamely. "How crazy is that?"

"And white roosters and a baby bear. The poor little bear got drunk on champagne. It was all written about in a famous Russian novel," I said. "It was called *The Spring Ball of the Full Moon*."

"Isn't that wonderful," Anna said. "I can just picture it."

Missy said something that sounded like: Wonderful.

I think I stayed long enough, to show whatever it was I thought I needed to show. I kissed Missy goodbye and shook hands with her sister and waited in the front hall while they rounded up the daughters, who waved from the stairs. I got back in my car and thought, Jesus Christ, please let me never complain again, about anyone or anything.

PART THREE

Remembrance Has a Front and a Rear

We came back from our northern holiday, more in love than when we'd left. People could see it a mile away. People asked Eleanor if she'd changed her hair. They told me I'd lost weight. We acted like people who'd leaped off the shipwreck just in time, and found themselves on a desert island with sunshine, shelter, and plenty of pineapples. I smiled when I saw other reporters. I could live without the bylines, easy. The night we came back, we were invited to a big lesbian dinner party with some of Eleanor's old friends from Mademoiselle Souvestre's boarding school. Your debut, Eleanor said. There were married ladies with a wandering eye and Eleanor's Seven Sister friends in Harris Tweeds and jaunty walking sticks (silver swan handle, are you kidding me) and elegant English walking shoes (Lobb's, the woman next to me said, holding up her foot, like I should sail right over and order a pair). One woman was divorced and after two martinis, she said she was as happy on the day they got divorced as she was when they got married and maybe more. Eleanor looked down at her plate.

Everyone talked about whichever girl they'd had a crush on in boarding school. Eleanor had been the reigning princess at Allenswood, which apparently made me every junior girl who laid flowers at her feet, screamed for her on the hockey field (where I would have kicked her ass, I'm pretty sure), and made her bed for her while she was brushing her teeth. The women laughed and clinked glasses: Here's to mad passion and pash madness. Eleanor squeezed my hand, in front of everyone, which was not a small thing, and then she said, Oh, Dearest, you know what English boarding schools are like. I sat up straight, representing my people, the hired girls of South Dakota, and I said, Oddly enough, I have no idea at all about boarding schools, English, French, or Fuck All. The prettiest woman from the old boarding school days coughed up her champagne and everyone pounded her on the back. Someone asked me what I did and Eleanor broke in to tell them I was Harry Hopkins's right-hand man, and there was suitable tittering. I was invited to describe the terrible things I'd seen in our great country, by two women who did care, and by women who were on their third glass of champagne, and then there were strawberries and cream and then we went back to the White House and we made love but we didn't talk.

For two years, I took my job for the Federal Emergency Relief Administration seriously. I traveled across the country and wrote to Eleanor and to Harry Hopkins every week, about the Depression: women dying in city hospitals, lying in the corridors, four in a row, piss and shit dropping to the floor, like they were so many cows. If they were poor enough and one of the adults was able enough, they could do the work some pencil pusher thought they should do, for a wage that didn't upset the local businesses. Farmers watched their babies get through the flu, survive mumps and measles, and then die of just plain starvation, before they turned two. Small boys and girls, still a little unsteady on their feet, pulled sugar beets from dawn to dusk. Gray-faced women tried to tidy their shacks the way my mother had: sweep the dirt out to the yard, watch it drift back in like a grim brown tide, wet two cloths, tie one over your hair and forehead, and use the other one to clean the sills and clean the table so you could make some kind of meal without the dust and cottonwood filling your mouth.

A girl, skinny and still flat-chested, saw my fedora and my coat and smelled my cigarette. She said, Mister, I costs you a dime. I said, It was all right, I'd give her the dime if she went home. She put out her filthy hand for the dime and walked up to the next corner, making sure I wasn't following and cutting into business. I stayed in a tent village in the Ozarks and saw a river of sewage cut a path down the middle of a dirt road. I stood in rubber boots at the edge of the water and I had to go back to my car when the toughest little boy, my shirtless hero, started fishing things out with a stick and a hairpin. He made a pile and stood guard over it, so when he was done, he could wash it in the lake two miles away and then, as he told me, he'd sell it maybe, or anyways, something for his sisters. I had my nose rubbed in my own racialism so often, and so hard, by meeting colored people who were so much worse off and had been hard done by for so much longer. Negro men and women, working from can to can't, surrounded by a sea of hungry, wide-eyed children and at least one rail-thin, night-dark old lady in the corner, sitting like a seer in her one dress, all knowing that their suffering registered less, that their dead weighed less, that there was less chance they could climb out of this terrible canyon, and fewer people to reach for them as they did. I finally had to give it up and it hurt me, I tell you, to understand that the Hickoks of Bowdle, South Dakota, with shoes from a dead girl to wear on school days only and oatmeal for dinner, were lucky people.

I Have No Life but This

....

Saturday morning, April 28, 1945
29 Washington Square West
New York, New York

We'd napped, rolling over to find each other. I reach for her before I open my eyes. She's in the living room, reading already. She looks up and smiles. She doesn't put up her arms for me.

"I've been reading for an hour," she says. "There's more tea. And a letter from Missy LeHand's nieces. And one from her brother."

Two years ago, I was living down the hall from Eleanor. We'd had a modest wartime Christmas. No rubber, no metal, no sugar, no butter. Eleanor and I exchanged gifts (a check from her, a blue scarf I got from the Democratic National Committee and put in a new box for her) in her room and we walked downstairs for cocktails, chaste as sisters. Franklin held up a cocktail shaker and a letter from Anna LeHand. Anna LeHand had written to Franklin that Missy was a wreck. She spelled out every detail of Missy's infinite misery and finally Franklin said it was a damned shame and he'd invited Missy to come for a week's visit, as soon as she was up for it. Eleanor nodded pleasantly and pointed out that there was not a single empty bedroom. Franklin waved his hand, to show how little this detail mattered. Three days later, Missy's sister wrote back to say that this was the best possible news, that Missy was very excited and when could she bring Missy down? Franklin handed the note to Eleanor and Eleanor had Tommie write to say regrettably, it wasn't possible at this time, but they would, of course, reschedule.

Missy's sister made damned sure the visit was rescheduled because she loved her sister and hoped to God that they could get out of Somerville and claw their way back to important meetings and White House dinners, with evening gowns and matching jackets, but it was canceled again, while I was out of town. Only Eleanor could have done that. I doubt Franklin thought any more about Missy and if she had come, she'd have been Eleanor's problem then too. I only knew because Grace Tully had no one else to tell.

On July 31, 1944, Missy's sister wrote, furiously, that they'd gone to the movies. There was a newsreel of the president and Missy rose unsteadily in the middle of it and announced to the theater that she needed to go home, immediately. That night, she took out all of her albums and letters from Franklin and laid them on her bed. She opened every page to a picture of him. She had a stroke, and called out his name and fell onto the pile. She was forty-eight. Not old.

Franklin was on his way to Alaska. Bill Bullitt was in Naples. None of the Roosevelt children came, except James's ex-wife, Betsey the starlet, who chatted up Eleanor at the interminable wake.

Eleanor and I, and the old postmaster general, Jim Farley, and Bishop Cushing and Judge Frankfurter, both of whom knew what was what, and young Tip O'Neill and vile Joe Kennedy came to the funeral at Mount Auburn Cemetery in Cambridge. Eleanor and I sat while the statement from the White House press secretary was read. The White House emphasized *faithful* and *painstaking*. Franklin hadn't seen her for almost three years. He found a few different ways to say it was a great thing, the way she'd laid down her life for his, with selfless efficiency. He said she had a real genius for getting things done. By which he meant, things for him. The cigarette, the blanket, the cushion, the prompt arrival of the presidential car, preceded by her deflecting everyone's attention from the quick carry of the president down a back stair. Missy was a genius at shining the light just so. She delivered the notes indicating yes when everyone in the White House knew the answer was, and always would be, no. The press secretary wrote: *Faithful and painstaking, with charm of manner inspired by tact and kindness of heart, she was utterly selfless in her devotion to duty. Hers was a quiet efficiency, which made her a real genius in getting things done. Her memory will ever be held in affectionate remembrance and appreciation, not only by all the members of our family but by the wide circle of those whose duties brought them into contact with her.*

There's a large rock nearby with a bronze plaque that simply reads LeHand and Missy's buried next to her sister, nowhere near Hyde Park. The Roosevelts paid for the funeral and her headstone carries a quote from that press release, like a letter of reference. *She was utterly selfless in her devotion to duty. Franklin D. Roosevelt.*

I don't think she would have liked more visits from me. There was nothing I could bring or say that would have helped. Eleanor and Franklin paid for the casket and the blanket of red and white flowers that covered it.

He ate her, I said to Eleanor, on the drive home. For twenty years. Those were the bones.

Oh really, Hick, Eleanor said.

Good Night, Sweetheart

....

Eleanor passes me more letters and begins reading one aloud. This is from Parker Fiske, she says.

She waves a large white envelope marked *Eleanor Roosevelt*.

"It says, 'Deliver to Eleanor Roosevelt in the event of my demise.' Do you think Parker's dead?"

Eleanor had taken lessons to get her high, fluting voice under control, which she almost has, and now, when she's distressed, she sounds like a bored radio announcer from Illinois.

I say, "If he died in the last three weeks, we would have heard about it. I'm sure he's fine." But even if he's not dead, I don't think he's fine. By the time we got to know each other, Parker was never fine. "You could call White Horse Hill, if you're worried," I say.

She cleans her glasses and reads to me.

18/4/45
White Horse Hill Manor
White Horse Hill, Maryland

Dear Eleanor,

I am so sorry. The loss of Franklin is as terrible to me, as the loss of my own mother was. I can only imagine how dark these days have been for you. But I know you. I know every time one of us stumbles to express how sorry we are for your loss, you'll say the right thing. In fact, I'm sure you've had to say it a hundred times, to all sorts of people, to every simpering Roosevelt cousin (I know you will find it unkind for me to say, but that flock that followed him, that gaggle of admirers seemed to have been chosen entirely for their ability to fawn without pausing for lunch), and to the haberdasher from Missouri. You put your hand on every shoulder and you tell them that you are, in your turn, very sorry for them. You are kindness itself but in that sweet, fluting tone there's more than a hint of: If I can pull myself together, dear, surely you can too.

You are kindness itself. You have never once spoken of my meetings with Miss Hickok but I feel sure that she told you about them. I would say that it was not my finest moment, but that list of not-fine moments is quite long. I have to add to them tonight. By the time you get this, I hope I'm dead.

Eleanor looks up over her glasses.

"I doubt it," I say.

"You had a conversation, you had conversations, with my cousin Parker Fiske. About what?" she says, in exactly the tone Parker Fiske was writing about.

He was a tall, lean, mean, well-dressed man. He had a long, disdainful face and steel-frame spectacles. He never looked out of place at the White House. He looked like what he was, a Roosevelt cousin, a page at their wedding, a famously deft, much-married diplomat who knew how to wrestle other countries into agreements. He looked like a man who knew how to ride horses and which fork to use and how to properly address the younger brother of a duke—and he was. He didn't look like a man who propositioned working-class men, white and black, in every possible conveyance (I'm just remarking that this stuff took place on trains, in cabs, in horse-drawn carriages, in the back of limousines, and on cruise ships, barges, and large sailboats). I think that's what almost saved him and that's what brought him low. People didn't see his homosexual self coming (unlike yours truly) and that bothered them. He didn't look at all like that type of man, so everyone who liked him—smart and charming and so good at his job—pretended it didn't happen, or that somehow it had happened but only due to a mix of bourbon and misunderstanding. I don't know what kind of misunderstanding it could have been. (No pussy down there? My mistake, sir.) The only time I ever heard Franklin refer to it, nothing was explained.

Franklin was presiding at dinner one night, in '33, when Amelia Earhart was our new best friend and Eleanor and I were in the throes. We'd dressed each other, to the nines (her in Eleanor blue, with navy piping, and me in navy silk with Eleanor blue at the waist). We each wore a white orchid on our right lapel. Honestly, you couldn't miss us. Dinner with other people, then, always left us restless and giddy, like thoroughbreds before a race, but dinners with Franklin wore me out. He was the handsomest man in every room and he was president. He always had Missy by his side, and sometimes another pretty woman or even a pair, seated near him, for no reason except to please his eye. I appreciated the pretty girls, the way I appreciated a nice vase or a very good but not great painting. Eleanor did too. We didn't aspire to it. We admired it.

When we were young women, there was fear and envy for her, desire and worry for me, but we got older. If you wait, everyone gets tired and the glittery gifts people carry will mostly be tossed aside just so they can cross the finish line. We both liked pretty women well enough, for different reasons, but by fifty, neither of us envied them.

"You cannot fault a man for what he does when he's intoxicated." Franklin meant Parker Fiske. Fiske wouldn't have to resign for another ten years but people were talking about him.

Eleanor said, "Really."

I said, "Do the ladies also get a pardon?"

I hoped Franklin thought so, but it didn't matter. Eleanor didn't think so. Eleanor thought that if you were a person of advantages and intelligence, you were responsible for every single thing you did or said and every choice you made until the day they laid you in the ground. That's how she lived her whole sainted life. If Eleanor had been Franklin, I would have worried about infidelity. I would have known that I was married to a charming liar. I wouldn't have been able to stand how easily she'd tell me one thing on Monday and another on Tuesday, without a blush.

Eleanor has only one face and it's the face I love most in the world, but for the day-to-day business of being human, Franklin was easier.

Amelia was in great form that night, sitting across from her idiot husband, George.

Amelia said, "You can't possibly mean that, Mr. President. In vino veritas, after all. We show our true colors, however unattractive, when we're drunk."

"Exactly," Franklin said, and he raised his coffee cup, to show that dinner was over, and wheeled off, laughing like hell.

Amelia turned to Eleanor and me and said, "That's why I don't drink, do I, G.P.?"

G.P., George Putnam, went to Harvard and married society ladies before and after Amelia. He owned three cars and five horses and four tuxes (I know because he told me) and still, sitting across from Amelia, who glittered like a wicked fairy, George looked like the poor fisherman in the folktale who'd gotten his wish and lived to regret it. He nodded, glumly. Nothing wrong with a drink once in a while, he mumbled.

Amelia said, "I think women—some women—regard matrimony as a highly honorable retreat from the possibility of failure in the larger world."

I said, Maybe some women, and Eleanor drank her water and Amelia kept talking.

"After all, it's nothing more than an attractive cage and some of us, we have to spread our wings, don't we, my dears?"

She winked at Eleanor. She lifted her pretty arms, under her sheer, spangled chiffon wrap so it slid to the floor, and George picked it up for her. She managed to make me sorry for him.

"Please finish Parker's letter," I say. "Then we can talk."

Eleanor looks at me over her glasses and reads to me, quietly, without inflection.

I was lying in a ditch, in my robe and pajamas, earlier this evening. I plan to go back there when I finish this letter. The ditch runs across the ass end of the property, behind the last row of cypress trees and yews. I tripped over the roots of an old maple tree and slid, ass over teakettle, into the ditch, and lay there, wedged in the dirt, like a soldier at Ypres.

I confess to you, I threatened the butler tonight. He threatened me. He stood on the other side of the kitchen table, white apron wrapped as tight as a cummerbund around his waist, shirt starched like a sheet of ice, and his cuffs rolled up to show his revolting monkey wrists. We'd had a drink together. I was tired and put my hand on Bauer's shoulder as I sat down. He didn't move away.

I remember this the way I remember much of the past— through a smoky bourbon haze. That's how I remember my first honeymoon, when I'd found myself—in black-and-white-striped silk dressing gown and some sort of French lounge pants plus silver-plated cigarette holder and not a shred of humor about my whole getup—in a suite of the Grand Hotel de Vesuvio in Milan. The bellman took his time unpacking our bags and when my first wife, Deborah, went into the large and beautiful bathroom, he hung up my jackets and my trousers, smoothing the legs. He looked at me, running his slim, tan fingers round and round the waistband of my suit pants until Deborah came out again, her hair fixed, her dimples showing.

That evening, I wandered—which is how I liked to think of myself then, a diffident traveler making his way through unfamiliar terrain—oh, la, who knows what I'll find behind this tree—into the dusty basement. There was luggage, a coat-rack, a bench and a sprung armchair, a dozen brooms, a row of grimy but uniform dustpans, and the beautiful boy. I extended our visit and for years Deborah would tell people, Say what you want about Florence and Rome, Parker and I adored Milan.

In the kitchen tonight, I told Bauer I'd give him the bottle, if he could beat me in arm wrestling. He nodded. I have longer arms; the better fulcrum and I beat him twice, nearly coming out of my seat to do it. I felt his warm, wet hand in mine, his arm under me. I said, Ich habe gewonnen! And he bowed his head a little. We clinked glasses and just as I thought things were going as smoothly as they could, that I would not find myself miserable and alone in my big bed, he stood up. He put his hand on my head and guided it toward his crotch. I pushed his hand away and stood up. I said that it was time for us to call it a night. I said there had been a misunderstanding. He didn't stand aside and I gave him a shove, just to clear my way. I was very tired.

Cybele came into the kitchen with a small bag and her big fur. She nodded to Bauer and smiled at me, as if we were in a lovely room, not a depressing kitchen. She looked me in the eye, so as not to look at anything else, and said that she was going to visit friends. I said that the roads were getting bad and that was enough. She pushed up her sleeves, ready to box, and said that there could be snow, hell, or high water on the roads tonight but she wasn't staying in the house with me, in the mood I was in. I said I wouldn't have another drink until Memorial Day. She said, You couldn't pay me to go through another day with you. We had reached that point.

I followed her into the front hall and watched her put on her coat. I tried a few husbandly gestures—my hand on her elbow, steadying her with the boots, pushing forward to lift her bag into the car. She ignored me. She walked to the car and left the front door open. The blue Chrysler pulled away, snow spraying, taking a big slide to the right. I watched until the twin tire prints were covered.

I fell asleep in the library and woke up to Bauer putting on his overcoat, knocking things over in the front hall. He carried his suitcase.

"You don't have to leave," I said. "It's coming down hard."

"No longer," he said.

He opened the door. Cybele's tracks were gone entirely. The dark night air dotted with flakes, and fresh as a forest. Bauer walked out and got into a beat-up Dodge sedan. The driver tapped his horn.

I should have said something conciliatory. I should have taken Franklin's approach and made a joke out of it, as if nothing serious had passed at all and only a fool would think it had. I'm famous for reconciling opposite parties, all over the world. I have no conciliation left in me. I want to be loved, the way my dear mother and my first wife loved me, and if I can't have that, I want to be desired fiercely. I want a man who will find me and never lose me. I have found that man, as it turns out, and the day before Christmas I told him we could never see each other again.

It's not our habit to be candid with each other but I would like, even if it's just while I'm writing, to imagine that I'll send this and that you'll know who I really am and you'll love me still. I would like, for this little while, not to be in disguise, and I like to imagine that at least while you're reading this, you are not in disguise, either. These days, you are usually disguised as First Lady. Sometimes, when I see you in those drafty halls, I hardly know you. Franklin himself was disguised only by his health. His performance as a man who had difficulty walking was one of the greatest performances of the twentieth century. To see him standing with his cane, leaning into the wind, hatless and defiantly cheerful, was to deny even the passing thought that if he'd had no strong man by his side, he would have fallen to the ground, instantly.

On a more cheerful note, I've been looking at pictures from your wedding this evening. I remember every detail of your royal wedding. I know, we both know, how the world came to see Franklin but back then, Franklin was a bit of a stiff and not much of an athlete. He didn't get into a good club at Harvard. He joked around like a missionary and drank like a guilty altar boy. And didn't he overcome both, con brio. The man married you and devoured Charm.

They put me in a page's suit for your wedding. Those were the days of mountains of ferns, allées of white ribbon, fields of white Prince of Wales ostrich feathers tipped with silver (the other Roosevelts' obsession with their ridiculous coat of arms), and pink roses everywhere. Among Roosevelts, you could not escape roses. Cousin Alice, no prettier than you, less clever, and so much worse a human being, did the same at her wedding. There were pale pink roses by the bushel, down the staircase, in the bridesmaids' bouquets, in those silver urns the size of a large child, and across the mantels of Sissy Parish's two drawing rooms. Your bridesmaids came down the stairs, perfecting their sulky, virginal sway down thirty-four steps.

I was twelve. I was bubbling over, sweating and smelling, breaking out in small red patches, on my chest and my cheeks. You turned around and gave me one of your sweet smiles. Just as I was about to pick up your train, my mother darted forward, with rice paper. She patted my face, to mop up what she could, and she smoothed my hair, which was standing up like pokeweed.

My mother was really very fond of you. She said that Grandma Mary Hall dragged you home from France and your feminist hotbed for no reason but polite society. Eleanor does not complain, she said. I complained, all the time. I even complained about having to be a page and wear a cravat but I was proud of it, and of my job, carrying the train. I complained about having to walk behind your grandmother Mary. Your grandmother managed, like a lot of rich old people—and I find that I am just like this—to insult people and take offense in the same sentence. She told me I was not to get in your way and when I rubbed my nose, just for something to do, she patted her chest and said that she hoped I wasn't suggesting that there was anything wrong with the air in the apartment, that she had not thought she'd be

*insulted by a weedy little boy on the morning of her grand-
daughter's wedding.*

*Both women were in black, both smelled like camphor and
attar of roses. I can smell it now, that acrid, biting scent
overpowering a dull, wistful one. I was twelve. I believe that
homosexuals are born, not made, but if I'm wrong, it was those
old ladies that turned me.*

*Your Uncle Teddy led us all into the reception and told story
after story. The men who liked him roared. The women sparkled.
Aunt Edith smiled behind her fan. Hall and I found the spiked
punch and took it into the back garden, drinking cupfuls as fast
as we could, until my father found us. My father smacked me on
the back of the head. He pulled Hall up and said, Your sister
relies on you, and Hall vomited into the chinaberry.*

*When we were both about to graduate from Harvard, Hall
took me to a show. That night was his gift to me. An enormous
man swung overhead, his feet almost grazing my head. He was
twice the size of Uncle Teddy, if you'll forgive me, in a black
bathing costume and bare feet and his thighs and backside
splayed out and hung over the seat. He grabbed on to the leather
straps of the swing with big hands and I could see that
underneath the black suit was another, red-striped suit. Sweat
ran down his sides. The man pumped his legs and tossed red silk
flowers into the audience. He must have weighed three hundred
pounds. He wore a straw hat, a boater, like all our uncles and
cousins wore at picnics, and his calves were like bowling balls,
white-blue and very smooth.*

*A few weeks before the nightclub debacle, I'd made a picnic
for Hall and me. We went down to the Charles and found one of
those great willow trees, its soft branches pooling on the grass. I
suggested we sit inside the canopy and he laughed.*

"That's baloney. Let's get some sun."

He took off his shirt and socks and shoes and rolled up his trouser legs. I took off my sweater and folded it beside me. Two boys we knew rowed by and they whooped. Hall jumped up, waving, and waggled his hips at them. His feet were beautiful. The toenails were smooth and rosy and each round, sturdy, clean toe had a couple of tiny gold hairs on it. We sat on the lawn, overlooking the river, drinking ale, eating apples and sausage rolls I'd stolen from the kitchen. That was my great daring. That's all I was capable of.

His pants hiked up his shins and I could see more gold hairs, a little darker, above his sharp white perfect anklebone. You know what a handsome young man he was, in his twenties. My feet, like every other part of me, were disgusting to me. I'd mastered the manly art of never being naked, and of appearing not to notice anyone else's nakedness—I don't know if that's how it is in girls' schools. I knew I looked nothing like Michelangelo's David or any of the sculptures in our art books or the statues in Auntie Bye's garden, where she refused to put up fig leaves and said that if anyone was so uncultured as to be offended, they should just close their ignorant eyes. We could use more of that.

That nightclub was heaven and hell for me. Lipsticked men danced together. An actual girl, looking like Mary Pickford, except for her backless pinafore, offered Hall a pink rose, for fifty cents. He put it in his lapel and sent her away. The big man from the swing had put on a silk dressing gown, leather boots on his bare legs, and a monocle. He did look like Uncle Teddy and he was not unaware of the resemblance.

"Oh, it's a bully night, isn't it, my dears. Bully, bully, bully. I see you little Rough Riders, out there. Daddy sees all. And now, lock your lips and hide your slips, because here to show you how to speak softly and carry a great big stick, and also, vicey-versy, here is Miss Gladys Bentley—"

People yelled and clapped. A Negro woman came in, large and handsome, in a white tux and top hat. She chucked men and women under the chin. She nuzzled a white girl, who screamed with pleasure. Two boys fanned themselves. She hammered at the piano, like it was her last night on earth, and while she sang in her deep, whiskey voice, two very pretty girls, one light, one dark, climbed onto the baby grand and sang back-up: "Blow it up right, with my own dynamite. I'm knocking down this city, knocking it all down tonight." Hall cheered. I clapped politely, coward that I was, and am. Hall pushed me toward every invert he saw. I stood my ground and finally sat down at the table nearest the coat check.

"Look," he said. "Let's have a ball. This place, it's great."

I asked him, grousing all the way, if he'd been here before.

"You goop. Who am I going to go with? Margaret? No, this is for us. This is our bachelor's party, without the rest of the fellows. Our send-off."

He didn't say, the rest of the fellows who don't care for you. The rest of the fellows who understand perfectly well what lies beneath.

One boy, without lipstick and dressed much like us, approached me. Hall was very warm but I think the boy must have seen that my strongest wish was to murder him and he shrugged. He said to me, Suit yourself, petal.

I grabbed my jacket, threw the tie in the coat check girl's face, and headed for my apartment. Hall ran out behind me but couldn't catch up. I didn't speak to him for the next three weeks and when he got married the first time, I was in Paris, myself.

The snow's stopped entirely.

When my mother died—and thank you for that lovely letter. I have kept it in a chest, along with some other letters that matter to me—I thought there was no worse pain.

There are people you always love, no matter what they have done to you, no matter what you have done to them. I think Miss Hickok is one of those people for you. I hope so. When you are the kind of man I am, you get to envy wives and husbands, the Franklins and the Eleanors. And now, I get to envy the Hickoks as well.

By the time you read this, I hope that Scotch and this deep snow will have put an end to me.

My dear Eleanor, I am so sorry about Franklin. He cast light, everywhere. Please forgive me for my deceit and my weakness. Forgive me, further, if you can, for attempting to interfere with your happiness. I want you to have happiness.

Your cousin,
Parker Fiske

The Show Is Not the Show

. . . .

SATURDAY NOON, APRIL 28, 1945
29 Washington Square West
New York, New York

"You and my cousin spoke," Eleanor says. "More than once?"
She's like a dog with a bone. Here's where Franklin would
make one of his lousy martinis and tell a joke but it's too early to
drink.

Parker Fiske and I met from time to time and after that, we sent
each other notes, and sometimes books (three years ago, we sent
each other *The Heart Is a Lonely Hunter* and he sent me a postcard
of Siamese twins, as a thank-you). Last year, he sent me an old
map of South Dakota, with dragons and tumbleweeds he'd
sketched around the edges. He signed the back, Your pal, Tom
Sawyer.

The first time we met, in 1934, he'd sent a note to my office, saying
that he'd be waiting for me in the coffee shop across the street
from the Mayflower Hotel, my home away from House then.

Maybe he knew I was sleeping in the White House. Lots of people did. Sometimes, I got mail there. We had our performance of Miss Lorena Hickok, friend of the family, coming for breakfast or dinner, which sometimes required me to slip out and stroll back in. Sometimes, for laughs, I'd tie my scarf differently, or pin a brooch to my hatband. Voilà.

He stood up when I came into the coffee shop and before I could order my coffee, he introduced himself.

"I do believe we've met before," he said. "Two Christmases ago, at the White House."

He lifted his hat. He put his hand on my elbow and said, "Would you care to join me?"

He stretched out his long legs until his shoes touched mine and then he stretched a little farther, so I pulled my legs under me.

"Good of you to come."

"I admire your work in the State Department," I said.

"And yours here at home. You must be just back from your sojourn among the good people of the Dust Bowl and places beyond."

"Just back."

He waved the waitress over and she poured us both coffee.

"I understand the reports you're doing for the Emergency Relief are excellent. Even Republicans weep over them. Pie?" he said. Meaning, obviously a great big creature like yourself eats pie every chance she can get.

"Oh, no," I said. "A cup of joe will be fine."

"Ever the reporter. Well, in a manner of speaking. I understand that your special friendship made journalistic objectivity impossible. All of Washington understood your dilemma. You made an honorable choice."

I sipped my coffee. (All summer, I'd been running into Louis Howe, Franklin's consigliere, roaming the White House halls in nothing but his boxers and a towel over his shoulders like a small, nearly naked vampire. He'd see me near Eleanor's room at all hours and say, Well, ain't *that* a scoop.)

"Well, honorable. That may be a little much. I mean, you are *shtupping* the First Lady. She is a married woman."

I choked on my coffee and I took my time, wiping my saucer, patting my blouse, and waving off the waitress so I could think about Parker Fiske threatening me and speaking Yiddish. A special friend had taught me Yiddish for every occasion, *shtupping* included.

"Mr. Fiske, we don't know each other very well. . . ."

It was true. I wasn't sure where I was going with it, but it was true.

"I don't know you, personally," he said. "I am familiar with your ilk. And I am more than acquainted with the great lady of whom we are speaking. I was a page at the President and First Lady's wedding. I am their cousin and it pains me to think, I shudder to think, what the President would say, if he were to hear about the filthy byways into which you have pulled his wife." He dropped his voice on the word *wife*.

"You can stop shuddering," I said. "He knows."

"He does not."

"Well, I say he does and I say he won't appreciate hearing what is either nasty gossip or an unpleasant fact or maybe not even that, coming from you. I know your ilk too, buddy. What's your point? That Franklin doesn't know and if he did, there'd be hell to pay? Divorce? Not going to happen. Disgrace? Not just my disgrace, pal. You know how men feel about having their wives stolen. And by a broad like me? I mean, it certainly wouldn't be fair, if Franklin killed the messenger, but I can see it, can't you?"

He shook his head.

"Let me take a different approach. Your relationship with the

First Lady is a thing of beauty. I don't wish you any harm, not at all. I thought we might have a mutual interest. I thought we might share information. I might tell you things, you might tell me things."

"What kind of things?" I said.

"So many people come and go in the White House. There might be some visitors that would be of interest, to some of my own friends. And my own friends, let's not say any one person's name here, this one very powerful friend has no wish to look closely at you and your special relationship. You are a patriotic American. The First Lady is, of course, a great American. There might be some people who come calling upon her, who even wish to exploit her, and you might, from time to time, as a friend to our powerful friend, pass on names, of people whose presence is . . . notable. Interesting. Just that. Just that."

There was a part of me that thought, This is not the worst deal. Comfort the afflicted—me—and afflict the comfortable, as Mr. Dooley used to say. Furthermore, when I was a reporter, I blackmailed people a hundred times to get them to give me what I needed. "Oh, Mrs. Jones, we're printing Mr. Jones's side of the story tomorrow. Don't you want a chance to tell yours? Gosh, I know I would. . . ." Parker Fiske said we would protect Eleanor and the rest of the country. I did love Eleanor and I did love my country.

I made myself stand up, like a person with integrity.

"Thanks for the coffee," I said.

He left and I slid my coffee over the bill, for the tired waitress. She came by. "Not your fella?"

"Not on a bet," I said.

She took me in. "Didn't think so."

I went to the ladies' room and threw up. What Parker should have said was, I'll tell Franklin that I know for a fact that everybody's talking and that the President is facing an organized campaign of moral disgust. No divorce and no disgrace for the Roosevelts, just Lorena Hickok out on her fat ass and not another day or night or telephone call with the lady in question. That was always my fear. Not that Franklin would find out but that someone would persuade him that I'd overstayed my public welcome, that too many people, real people, Democrats who lived in small towns and Midwestern cities, seemed to know lesbian love when they saw it and they were seeing it now. If that's what Parker Fiske was threatening me with, and all he'd wanted was some gossip in return, I'd been a fool not to listen. I sat in the stall until the waitress knocked.

That night, Eleanor and I hardly saw each other. There were sixteen of us for dinner. Eleanor lifted a hand from across the room and I lifted mine back. The chances were pretty good that when the photo came out, in the *Post* or *The Telegraph*, I'd be cropped out of it.

Heaven Is What I Cannot Reach

....

SATURDAY NIGHT, APRIL 28, 1945
29 Washington Square West
New York, New York

Tonight, Eleanor and I are our dumb, happy, animal selves. We do our stretches (my hips, her back) and take our antacids, and we push and pull the pillows, in a comic performance of old ladies getting ready for bed. Whoever gets into bed first sets the mood, but what we do hasn't changed much from ten years ago. My hand's in her hair and her left hand is on my left hand. There is a great warm border between us and when things are the way they should be, she pulls my leg closer in behind her and I smooth her hair back from her forehead. We sigh. We give each other little kisses in odd places, the elbow, the shoulder, the chin. Years apart and other loves and still, I feel like my heart has at last, and only now, returned to my body. She rolled over onto me last night, in her sleep and said, I miss you, my dear. I said, I'm right here, and she said, insistently, I miss you, and put her chin on my shoulder. Right now, I love Eleanor more and more easily, at night, than I do during the day. Sometimes, I love her more when I don't even see her.

During the day, we are who we are and that's too bad. The

subject of Franklin the Person seems to be off the table. To keep the peace, I act as if Franklin and I were great pals and, had he lived, we all would have come to a comfortable understanding. The war would end and he'd retire to Top Cottage (Blowjob Cottage, as I thought of it), his Hyde Park hideaway in the woods, away from mother and wife, alternating between the glamorous babes and the devoted handmaidens, and Eleanor and I would get Val-Kill, cozying up on the porch, in matching cardigans, with a pile of books to be read and thick notebooks, for the books we'd write. We'd wave to Franklin, when we saw him up the hill. When the kids came to visit, I'd step back. I'd have lunch in town and sleep in "my" bedroom, which I'd decorated in '36, making it look like the cell of a nun with a passion for the Dodgers and *The New York Times*. I kept an antique, ivory brush-and-comb set on the dresser. When Eleanor saw it she gasped. That was my aunt's, she said. It was in the attic, I said. I thought it made a nice statement. I've even brushed my hair with it. I put two shirts in a drawer and hung two old dresses in the closet, for show.

I never stopped envisioning every piece of that life to come; the two cottages, our dogs; the way, over time, the kids would come to see how happy I made their mother and what good care I took of her. We would keep the best of our friends. Our love would create its own world and alter the real one, just a little. I could see the stand of birch trees, at the edge of the stream near Val-Kill, a few yellow leaves falling in. I could see our breakfast, the scrambled eggs still steaming, the newspapers folded. I could hear the creak of the rocking chairs on the porch.

It is not true that if you can imagine it, you can have it.

Eleanor hasn't eaten all day. I offer her a sandwich, Scotch or sherry, crackers or her favorite muesli, and she keeps shaking her

head. When the children were small, she says, she barely ate for
five years, because of everything. (Everything, she says. Five children and the baby died and then Lucy Mercer. And I was being
such a fine, fair person and I thought, I will live with him and just
not love him and then he got polio. And I heard the door slam.)
It was so terrifying, she says, that she couldn't swallow.

"You'll never guess who tracked me down," I say.

Eleanor rolls over.

"Which girlfriend?" she says, flatly.

Eleanor's understanding of our relationship was that our remarkable kinship, our communing spirits, made it possible for us to
engage in physical intimacy, the likes of which she'd never known.
(Sorry, Franklin, but you learned absolutely nothing at Harvard
and not much from Lucy Mercer, who I imagine was the "You're
my hero" kind of sex partner. I'll just say that after the polio,
Franklin's own people spread the word that the man was para-
lyzed from the waist down and could now be officially held blame-
less with the ladies, no matter how it looked. There's a certain lack
of imagination among Roosevelt enemies and also, among the
Roosevelts themselves.)

For Eleanor, lovemaking had everything to do with a comming-
ling of souls. She felt this way about all happy couples—that
joyful sex had come their way because of their love and when the
sex faded away, their love would burn even brighter, because the
source of the fuel was now high, not low. I don't care why the light
burns. I think that even if you are both old ladies riding side by
side on the Second Avenue subway, with one of you going home
to three grandchildren and a doddering husband, you can lock
eyes, and remember when you weren't. You remember that very
pleasurable and surprising thing that was done to you by the

wrinkly old bag of bones next to you and you breathe in memory the weight and the mortality and the sensible shoes are just costume, falling away, and your real selves rise up, briefly, dancing rosy and naked, in the middle of the subway car.

"My sister Ruby," I say. "She saw my name in the papers, next to yours. First Friend," I say, and I poke her in the side. She brushes my foot away and sits up, as if I have finally said something worth listening to.

"I would love to meet your sister."

You will, I say, and I lure her into planning how to help Ruby, and then the rest of the world, into considering that there's more to life than the Widow of the Great Man. There's a whole third act, I say, schools and governments and whole continents, all longing for her. The story is not over, I say, no matter how many times she says that it is. And we can start with making a nice luncheon with Ruby Hickok Claff, who wasn't as sweet as she was in South Dakota, thirty years ago, but wasn't as soft either. Ruby did her research and came to see me at my Little House on Long Island. She knocked on my door and I didn't know her and she threw her arms around me. By the time we sat down for coffee, I could see she was disappointed that I didn't live a more glamorous life and she was more than disappointed to find out that I didn't even own the house. Everything I owned was my pots and pans, my clothes, my typewriter, two fresh ribbons and three reams of paper, my car, and my dog. I cooked a couple of meals for her and she slept on the couch. We got ready for bed and she told me how things had been for her in Wisconsin, with our mother's sister. Not really so bad, but I could have used you, she said. You looked out for me. She asked for a loan, which I expected, and I gave her twenty-five dollars, which was no small thing for me. She told me her husband was out of work and that she was thinking of starting her own cookie-baking business, if I'd stake her to it.

Eleanor loves hard-luck stories and we can start with Ruby.

PART FOUR

The Inundation of the Spring

· ·

Sunday noon, April 29, 1945
29 Washington Square West
New York, New York

Eleanor had asked me not to come to the funeral.

"It was a beautiful day," she says, over her sherry. "I cannot tell you how beautiful it was. Very sunny and bright. I don't think there was a cloud in the sky. Dearest, the lilacs. White lilacs. Can you imagine they were out already, so early. You should have seen those horses, all decked out. Pulling him up the hill from the train."

She wipes her eyes. I wipe mine.

"There were fighter planes overhead, in formation. I don't know who thought that was the right touch. Maybe it was. They did the twenty-one-gun salute. Fala barked."

"Twenty-one times?" I say, to make her laugh.

"I think so. I didn't notice much, besides the lilacs."

She slides down in the bed, back to the pillows, and curves around my hip. I look down at her and stroke her arm. Her skin has always been finer and softer than other people's. Other women's. It's like old silk now and the lines, the tiny diamonds traced on her skin, take nothing from the fineness.

"I should have had you come."

"It's all right," I say. "You couldn't do everything. Not even you. You had all those people to organize and comfort and your own grief. You didn't need to worry about me, on top of everything else."

"Are you quoting me?"

"Pretty much," I say. "I took it as a compliment." Which is what I said. When people asked, I told them that Eleanor didn't want her closest friends there. This funeral is for the whole world, I told them. She's going to do what must be done and she is going to do it beautifully. It's not really a private occasion, I said.

"I couldn't ask for you to be just one friend among many friends, one more face in the crowd while the whole world wept over Franklin. And the reception. I wouldn't have had five minutes to hold your hand. For you to hold mine."

"You could have asked," I say.

It was sunny on Long Island too, the day of his funeral. The lilacs were out there too. I took Mr. Choate for a walk in the woods in the morning and even deep in the woods, in the thick, shifting light playing on the dead leaves and pine needles, the bright green shoots and narrow tines of forsythia, the spreading damask moss and fat red buds, were all breaking out and up, subtle as a cartoon.

I came back and showered. I dried myself, without looking, and I patted myself all over with scented talc on a white-feathered powder puff the size of a frying pan. Eleanor had gotten me both last Christmas. War be damned, she said. In thirteen years, we'd only missed one private Christmas, and right then, that seemed promising. I pinned up my hair, and put on a clean shirt, my last remaining pair of the French silk panties, and gardening blue jeans. I sat at the kitchen table, watching the sky, wiggling my toes, trying to get more feeling in my feet. I ate oatmeal with almonds for breakfast, just so I could tell Eleanor I did. I looked at the bacon in my refrigerator and said, Not today, heart attack. I made coffee the way I liked it and tossed Mr. Choate a biscuit. I leaned against the counter, watching the clouds. I have been lonely in my life but never when drinking strong coffee, wearing my fleecy slippers, and standing in my own kitchen. By the time we saw each other, I'd have my diabetes back under control and we could stop talking about it. I did my ankle, knee, and hip circles. I did my shoulder stretches and listened to "Nessun Dorma." I sang "Nessun Dorma," which surprised the dog.

If you can be worried, hopeful, truly sad, and enjoying the weather, I was. Mastic was beautiful to me, all year long, but in late spring it was lush and tenderly green in every corner. My Little House, peeling white paint and a kitchen out of Dickens, was my first real home since I'd left South Dakota. The fact that I rented didn't change my feelings. Renting made it better. Some people like to travel light and like to rent, and I am those people. To have a little white house on someone else's pretty property, to enjoy someone else's boat or beach or great front porch and not have to fix any of it is a particular kind of pleasure for me.

Franklin and Eleanor were terrific owners of things. They were stewards of properties and collections and furniture that had been around for two hundred years. They had silver, they didn't buy it, was what people like that said. I had six forks and six knives and I always had eight dinner plates in case I went crazy and threw a couple. The day Franklin died, I walked to the beach, without the dog, and broke all I had. He was the greatest president of my lifetime and he was a son of a bitch every day. His charm and cheer blinded you, made you deaf to your own thoughts, until all you could do was nod and smile, while the frost came down, killing you where you stood. He broke hearts and ambitions across his knee like bits of kindling, and then he dusted off his hands and said, Who's for cocktails? If Missy's strokes hadn't killed her, Franklin's cold heart would have.

I planted pansies the morning of his funeral and worried. I worried for the country. I worried for our soldiers. I worried for the poor, and the Negroes. I worried for the Jews, who hadn't even been people to me, when I was a girl. Franklin didn't do much for them but he wanted them safe, even if most of America didn't give a damn, and I wasn't sure Harry Truman worried much about people who were not like Harry Truman. I was sorry for us all. Harry Truman was a decent man but he was not going to be chugging brandy at two A.M. with Winston Churchill, belting out "Marching Through Georgia." Harry Truman would, admirably, do what he said he would do, in his stubborn, guileless way, and he would at least get us through the end of the war. There wouldn't be two courts in the White House anymore, two full sets of chutes-and-ladders for those in the know, and even if cocktails were served, Harry wasn't likely to dress up as Julius Caesar and sing "I Get a Kick Out of You" and Bess Truman wasn't going to make an appearance in a home movie as a Victorian maiden struggling, but not too hard, to get away from wicked pirates. Mousy Mary Margaret Truman wasn't going to make headlines. Franklin was a terrible husband and an unnerving friend and my rival and my president. I had kissed him on his birthday one night and he had held on to my hand, pressing hard, and I was, for that minute, as in love with him as any of them.

He'd left us, in a half hour, between lunch and dinner, when we'd let down our guard and now we were all sick with grief. Those of us who knew him and needed him didn't want to stop grieving, for fear we'd step forward, toward the future, and entirely lose the trace, the smell, and the feel of him.

It's All Right with Me

. . . .

SUNDAY AFTERNOON, APRIL 29, 1945
29 Washington Square West
New York, New York

"Dearest?"

Eleanor takes another envelope from the gray canvas mailbag. It will be more love, more sympathy, and more requests for help, in the form of cash and favors, tucked into sympathy. I've gotten cash and I've gotten favors and I know better than to raise an eyebrow at even the baldest lie.

"Did I tell you?" she says. "I got a letter from Missy's sister."

"Anna LeHand? That's nice," I say.

Eleanor nods. I open the curtains and she shakes her head, to make me close them.

"Anna LeHand herself was not nice," I say. "You make me say these things. You make me say Anna LeHand wasn't nice. You won't say it, so I have to. I want to lie through my teeth. I'm sure Anna is still her envious, small-minded self and just a monument of resentment. The greatest moment in that woman's life must have been when that piece of shit Joe Kennedy put his hand on her knee at Missy's funeral."

"I don't make you say these things." Eleanor turns on her bedside lamp. She looks at me over her glasses. "You choose to. And here I sit, about to remark on your basic decency and clear-eyed compassion."

"You're killing me," I say.

We can, I hope we will, go back and forth like this all day. Her propriety, my brass knuckles. Her Hyde Park–iness, my South Dakota gloom. The Roosevelts cultivate Chin up and make the best of it. None of them ever see that what they're making the best of is tons of money, a tenement's worth of servants, and such a grand old name that it doesn't matter that two hundred years ago they were no better than the Hickoks of South Dakota, which is a damn low bar. Rich people.

Stacks of condolence notes, to read, or not read, are in every room, spilling over the coffee table, snaking down to the floor, up to and under the couch. The first night, we put hundreds of the ordinary-people ones right into the blue mail sack, for the secretaries Tully recruited. Eleanor loves the ones written in pencil, the ones where people have fashioned their own envelopes from another piece of paper and a little glue, and if you don't have glue, you line up the two corners, tear a little tab into the middle and fold it back. I wrote letters that way myself twenty years ago, freezing my ass off in the Battle Creek post office, scrounging for two-cent stamps, so I don't love them so much. The letters from the Most Famous People have already come. Churchill wrote and Eleanor said, I know he meant it. Stalin's letter was sentimental and terrifying. The State Department sent Eleanor the front page of *Pravda*, trimmed in black. Admiral Kantaro Suzuki broadcast his mysterious condolences from Japan. He offered his profound sympathy. He praised FDR's leadership in bringing our country to an advantageous position in the war. It was such an un-American thing to do, to express genuine admiration for the man responsible for firebombing your civilians, we almost took it as propaganda. Eleanor said, I think Japan and America will never understand each other.

Every minor royal joined in. Clementine Churchill's note is so elegantly heartfelt and well written, I don't even make a face when Eleanor reads it aloud to me, again, and says, as she does every time Clemmie's name comes up, What a lovely woman. So strong, so much more progressive than he is, that big baby. Clemmie has a good head on her shoulders, let me tell you. She's better than he deserves, she says.

"As people always say about you."

I bury my face between her shoulder blades. She reaches back to press my head to the base of her neck. This is the happiness I want. Not the tidal wave of early romance, swamping all the boats, carrying us to some impossible shore. I'm not looking for wildness, half-undressed beneath the gorgeous blizzard of cherry blossoms that covered us and our picnic, in the farthest corner of a Maryland park. I don't need another bruising, blinding sunset at Gaspé, fiery orange streaking over the green lawns and red cliffs, dropping into the dark sea and leaving us to feel our way along the path, her hand in my waistband, making the case that there's nothing for us to do but buy the cabin we're sleeping in and never go back. She caught my hand in the dark and said, We will live someplace just like this.

I hold on to a hundred secret candlelight dinners, a towel spread out on the hotel bed, plates on the nightstands and two decanters on the floor, sherry and Scotch. Two hundred secret lunches. Working on her speeches, with the windows open and the birds singing. Whole secret weekends, beginning at nine o'clock on a Friday night and ending before noon on Sunday. Every Friday night was Roman candles and every Sunday morning, a slow, sad gathering up until we found ourselves, sitting over tea, just waiting for the hearse of real life to come to the door at noon. In that first year of craziness, whenever we were supposed to be working, there'd come a moment when everyone else had stepped out of the room. Our reports and folders slid to the floor. Eleanor put her hand firmly on the doorknob and locked it and untied the bow at her neck.

"Could we?" she'd say.

I remember every time we made love. I remember the light on her body, on dozens of beds. I remember all the blankets because I remember her hair spread out on them, caught in the weave and the smell of mothballs at Campobello and the smell of the cucumber skin cream we both used one winter. I remember the satin ticking on the old wool blanket at my place on Long Island and her arms overhead, her fingers tucked under the stitching, gripping the wool. That's what I did at night, these last eight years of being demoted to First Friend. I remembered. I was still better off than poor dead Louis Howe, who had loved Franklin with his whole faltering, manipulative heart. I was no worse off than Tommie Thompson, my pal, the other priestess at the shrine of Eleanor. Tommie's beau, Henry, was as undemanding as a potted plant. I used to refer to him as Tommie's beard, but that wasn't fair, because what was being hidden wasn't sex of any kind, but a devotion that makes sex look like a short swim in a shallow pool.

The month of our final breakup was one long Alphonse-Gaston routine. No one could go first, so we didn't go at all.

Eleanor pretended that what she wanted, more than anything, was my happiness. If I complained about how little I saw her, or our long evenings with Earl Miller, her old bodyguard, and whichever wife he was married to, or my blood sugar or that the reporters dogged our every dinner out, it was all evidence of my unhappiness. Unhappy was not the kind of girlfriend Eleanor wanted. I could stop bitching about how little time we had and stop complaining about the gossip or I could stop being her Dearest in All the World. And I pretended that all I wanted was her happiness. And if she was worried about me, or my behavior, if she was fretting about my gallivanting or nagging me about my diet, or complaining that I hadn't come by in the fifteen minutes she'd allotted to me, well, then, she wasn't happy, either, was she?

With all the goodwill and dissembling in the world, we almost dumped each other a dozen times and still we couldn't part. We stated the facts, over multiple breakfasts. We made observations. We summed things up, neatly, which was just like lying, and we both said that we would never stop loving each other, which was, unfortunately, absolutely true. We were determined to be the people we wanted to be and not the blind, desperate people we were.

Every few days, I said we needed to talk, and every few days, she said the same thing to me.

One morning, Eleanor said brightly, "Franklin said you haven't been around much. He said he's missed seeing you."

I said, "We really do need to talk. Get your hat. We can take my car."

I drove to Rock Creek Cemetery, so we could sit under her favorite statue. We got out and Eleanor looked up at the big woman, grieving and almost peaceful, and she smiled a little.

"Oh dear," she said.

I said, "I love you. You love me. In another life, we would have the cottage or the school, or the townhouse, or whatever it is. But not in this life. Not in this life, Eleanor, and I'm not going to be the White House pet."

I called her Eleanor, to show I wanted a fight.

"What a thing to say. You're not a pet. You're part of our family."

I stood up and she shrank, a little.

"We could try. You could be patient, and when he's no longer president—"

"When he's no longer president, which will be the worst loss of his life, as bad as polio, you're going to leave him? I don't think so."

She put her hands on the base of the statue.

"I don't care what people say about us," she said. "And Franklin doesn't listen to gossip."

"Franklin has the greatest ear for gossip of any man I've ever known. He's heard plenty."

"Well," she said, "he has never raised any objection."

It was my turn to study the granite folds. Maybe it was all vanity, maybe it was only that I didn't want to be First Friend, barking but harmless, and truly housebroken. I didn't think there was any decent way to say that since I couldn't destroy her marriage, I had to retire from the field. Franklin had won, as he and I and Eleanor had fully expected, and I wasn't even entirely sorry. The country needed him and he needed her.

"I appreciate that," I said. "Dearest, I don't think I can be what you'd like me to be. I will always want—"

She didn't come to me. She sat on the bench and waited for me to finish.

"I will always want to be your lover. Your mistress. To have you be my mistress. However you put it, I don't actually want to be your dear friend. I want to have fights. I want to get jealous. Just a little. I want you to get jealous. I want to follow you into your room—"

She stood up and put her hands out.

"I wish you could love me a little less, in that way," she said. "Not less. I don't mean less."

"Yes, you do," I said. I jangled the car keys. "You know that Dickinson poem. *So we must meet apart, You there, I here, with just the door ajar . . .*"

"You know, Emily Dickinson had no husband, no children. She did not have to do what I have to do."

"You're right," I said. "You are right. About all of this."

We drove to the White House in silence. I would move out and back to New York. I would still come and go to the White House. She would write to me often and I would write a little less often. I'd counsel her about the kids, who mystified her, and she'd send me a winter coat for Christmas. She would say, Nothing has really changed.

By 1939, I was part of the White House menagerie, once more.

My finances weren't in great shape and Eleanor knew it. It so happened there was an empty room in the White House, as there usually was. It so happened that this room was not so close to Eleanor's as six years before but it wasn't so far away either, and of course, Eleanor offered it to me, and of course, I accepted.

I was included at meals, because it would be odd and revealing not to include me. Housekeeping tidied up my room. I wasn't asked about my needs or preferences, or why the hell I was there, because no one wanted to hear about why my presence was desired and despite everyone's relief that I was no longer First Friend, it was too bad that I wasn't entirely gone and it was upsetting to people that when I came into the room, Eleanor Roosevelt stopped whatever she was doing, as if there'd been a shift in gravity. She'd clear her throat and carry on, never looking anywhere near me.

I lived in the White House and wrote for money. I hustled hard doing PR for the New York World's Fair, all 1,216 acres of it, trying to make Flushing, New York, a place people would come to by choice. I wrote press releases and brochures day and night for the world of tomorrow. I wrote about the Eyes of the Fair (on the future) and the Fair of the Future (familiarity with today is the best preparation for tomorrow). I wrote about the Westinghouse Time Capsule, not to be opened until 6939, in which we'd put a Mickey Mouse watch, twenty newsreels, a fountain pen, a woman's hat (Lilly Daché), a slide rule, a pack of Camels, seeds for all kinds of crops, from carrots to cotton, some pages from Albert Einstein, and a book by Thomas Mann (I voted for Willa Cather, the great novelist, exemplar of chunky, no-nonsense Midwest womanhood). I interviewed the creators of Futurama and of Democracity. People closely involved with the fair tended to think of themselves as ancient, omniscient Egyptians or as visionary beings, coming back from the future to share it with the average American. I quoted the chairman of the board of Westinghouse, on opening day, when he said (with no help from me): "May the Time Capsule sleep well. When it is awakened five thousand years from now may its contents be found a suitable gift to our far-off descendants."

I ate lunch in the French Pavilion almost every day. I interviewed Jiggs, the trained orangutan, and all of the almost-topless ladies who modeled as Greek goddesses and Italian art. Franklin opened the fair with a televised speech about peace and our four freedoms and the next day, television sets, the greatest thing since the radio, went on sale. Eleanor loved it. Forty-four million people came to the fair and I was thrilled when it was over.

I pretended every day to be Eleanor's friend. I pretended to feel fond and calm, concerned but apart. There wasn't any room for what I did feel, which was a sort of furious shame, run through with terrible strands of hope. (This is not just the province of lesbians, I'm pretty sure. See: Eleanor, Missy, Lucy Mercer Rutherfurd, Anne Morrow Lindbergh, my mother.) I pretended that other women, especially Marion, prettier, sweeter, less high-hat and less self-righteous, were just what I was looking for, which they should have been. When there was no one else in my bed, I imagined, like all lovesick girls, that the pillow was Eleanor's face, that my folded quilt was the length of her, that the dog at the foot of my bed would break the spell and reveal herself to be the woman I was crying over.

Today, I'm putting my trust in the visible world: in our cups of coffee, our reading glasses, my insulin, her aspirin, our hairpins, our toast, hers dry, mine soaked with jam, and our pale, naked feet, calloused and bony, pressing against each other. I do know better. I know cups of coffee with our coral and red lipstick stains are no different, no more permanent, than the pink and white cherry blossoms that shook down on us one beautiful afternoon but I kid myself that if I skirt the mercurial and magic moments, the coffee cups and reading glasses will promise, and deliver.

"I'm thinking of making a sandwich," I say. "What do you hear from Joe Lash?"

This is not the smartest move on my part. Young Joe Lash is a thorn in my side. He is Eleanor's Princess Martha of Norway and if I said that, I'd find myself standing in the hall, holding my coat. Eleanor sighs and smiles at me for the first time this weekend.

"He wrote me a beautiful note. He's still in the Pacific. I do worry about Joe."

She worries about him all the time. She worries about him and reminds everyone about his brilliance and his dazzling principles and if Joe Lash is in Guadalcanal because Franklin had him sent there, well, thank you, Franklin.

"Of course you worry," I say, which is a pretty good alternative to what I think.

If Eleanor has to be infatuated with a man, I prefer Earl Miller, who'd been her devoted, bull-necked, chivalrous bodyguard. I do like Earl, most of the time. He's married a couple of times but he's always devoted to Eleanor, and nothing is beneath him. Joe Lash is devoted to Joe Lash. Earl Miller was Eleanor's knight. He flirted with her, just enough, and walked by her side, watching for varlets and puddles. If cloaks were in fashion, he would have laid his right down. Earl was some kind of masculine balm to Eleanor's hurt pride. You can see it in the photos. The man was always by her side, at her shoulder, not two inches between them. If he hadn't gotten her away from the kids and onto the tennis court and up the mountainside, hadn't kissed her hand and waltzed her around at parties, I don't think I would have had a chance. Earl opened the door and I walked in. I owe Earl. I don't think anyone owes Joe Lash anything and Tommie Thompson hates him more than I do, which is good. Tommie's dislikes run deep and if you aren't serving Eleanor, you are a worthless Republican, or possibly Communist, piece of trash in her eyes. So, compared to Tommie, I myself am Eleanor Roosevelt: open, tolerant, and determined to give every idiot the benefit of the doubt.

"I don't think you really appreciate Joe," Eleanor says.

"Maybe not. I like Trude. She's very nice. She impresses me. And I can see how Joe might be the kind of son you wanted."

I hope this is right. I certainly hope that late at night, alone in the mahogany bed, she hasn't been longing for his scrawny little arms around her. "He's Jewish. He's a real intellectual. Maybe a Commie. Definitely not a Roosevelt."

"You're right," she says and she goes into the bedroom and comes out barefoot and without a robe, which are both remarkable events, and she pads back into the kitchen.

"Does Joe know about us?" I ask. "As we were?"

Eleanor puts our two sandwiches on a plate and boils water for tea. She pretends not to hear me but because she is who she is, she can't stick with even this tiny lie of omission for five minutes.

"It's not that kind of relationship. It's not about who I am, it's about who he is. He *is* the son I always wanted. He thinks I should be president. He lets me dote on him. He lets me make a fuss over him. And I have really come to love Trude."

When Joe went into the Army, Eleanor made him a party at the Brevoort Hotel that was half coronation and half bar mitzvah. There was an eight-piece orchestra and Joe was radiant. He said he was honored and embarrassed and all of us old hands were polite. Earl was an inch away from inviting him to arm-wrestle.

"With Joe, there are no terrible stories of what I failed to do when he was six, or how I let him down when he was learning to drive, or how I've kept him from fulfilling his destiny."

I could say that Joe Lash seems to have a very firm grip on his destiny but I want our day to be wonderful and I want my tea.

"Joe Lash is very, very lucky to have you," I say. Her boys aren't bad but I wouldn't want sons like them either. The Kennedy boys are more likely to succeed because Joe Kennedy is a toad, a bully, and a thief and they'll be living down their old man all their lives. I don't say this. I carry everything to the table.

Eleanor kisses me on the mouth.

"Thank you," she says. "And thank you for keeping your mouth shut."

"Oh, you're welcome. I'm learning. And, frankly, Joe Lash does not know the real you," I say, looking for the right tone. "I do. Lazy. Capricious. *Republican*."

"The real me," she says. "Ooh-la-la. I believe *Time* magazine called me 'gracious, energetic, long-legged.' I'm delightful. *Time* magazine said so. And long-legged."

She leans back in her chair, putting her long, blue-traced legs up in the air and flexing her feet. I hear the bones snap and pop. I put my thick legs up and flex my feet too. We have two hammertoes, one bunion, and a little bit of gout, between us. We do the ankle circles her doctor recommended. Clockwise. Counterclockwise.

"Symphony in arthritis," I say.

She pokes me with her big toe and I stroke her smooth calf with my instep. We watch our feet and veined legs as if they're the best show since the Follies.

"I love this," I say. "We haven't done this in so long."

Eleanor props herself up on the cushions and strokes my arm. The little ring I gave her ten years ago catches the light.

"I haven't taken it off for weeks," she says.

The little sapphire ring was a fixture in the beautiful love letters Eleanor wrote me: "I say to myself, she must love me or I wouldn't be wearing it." I'd see the ring on her hand in newspaper photos, when we were apart, and the sight of it was like being kissed on the mouth. Later, after we declared that we were friends and nothing more, we wrote cool and friendly letters, in which she advised me on my diabetes and I asked after Franklin's health and neither of us could bear to say, How can this be the awful gray place in which we now live? Then, she one-upped me. I'd written with the sad news that Tini Schumann-Heink had died and I mentioned going to the opera with a new friend, as a way of celebrating Tini's life. Eleanor wrote back a long, solicitous condolence note offering to give my little sapphire ring back to me for safekeeping. Not, Oh, darling, what a loss for you, that magnificent woman who gave you such an exquisite education. Eleanor wrote two pages about the safety and security of the ring. Should she keep it in a vault? Perhaps she should have it delivered to me, where I could keep it safe in my pantry, my sugar bowl, the back of the icebox? I had so many people, such a large circle of friends, in and out of my shack, where would it be safe? You never lock your doors on Long Island and anyone, just anyone, could push the glass right through those sagging window frames with a strong arm, she wrote. I wrote back, wishing the ink was dripping acid, that the only value the ring had for me was on her hand. If it wasn't going to be there, she could give it to the suffering poor, whom I knew she liked so much, especially in the aggregate. She didn't answer that one and she didn't send the ring back.

I saw, as soon as she'd come in last night, that it was on her hand and so much less grand than I thought it was, when I was twenty-four. I'd thought then that it was a serious piece of jewelry, the kind of thing Gable would give Lombard and now I knew better. Eleanor rubbed it against her slip, to brighten it, and shrugged, as if it was too hard, or too sad, or too late, to say anything more about it.

Ernestine Schumann-Heink was fifty-five years old when I met her, silver hair in a bun, a collar of broderie anglaise, on top of ivory watered silk, edged around with sharp points of lace, buttoned with gold and ivory roses, topped off with a poof of silver hair under a huge white cartwheel hat, as iconic in its way as the Eiffel Tower. She put out her soft hands, pink-tipped and ivory under the white crocheted glove, and slid them forward beneath her coat's flounced sleeve, to clasp my hands. I didn't understand and she let me make a hodgepodge American butch half bow, half curtsy. I'd run through a Milwaukee rainstorm and managed to keep my wet felt hat on my head. I didn't acknowledge the water pooling under my cracked shoes. There wasn't a part of her that wasn't powdered or lacquered, corseted, draped, and ruched. I know now what it takes for a stout, middle-aged woman to look good and keep looking good, and I feel for her.

I couldn't take my admiring eyes off her. Eleanor would have found her ridiculous and vulgar but if you want to celebrate quiet good taste, don't invite poor people. I'd had enough dirt-colored cloth, plain lines, and ugly things whose function was obvious, to last me a lifetime. Eleanor used to show me pieces of rustic furniture from Val-Kill or Arthurdale, the way you'd show a Frenchman a pastry, I guess—as if just his pedigree made him a good judge of the thing. I hated every just-plain-folks piece of it and when Franklin said he'd pay good money to see even one comfortable armchair come out of either place, I agreed. I suggested William Morris fabric, because it was the most expensive I'd ever heard of, and I suggested it'd be nice to have table legs you wouldn't split a shin on.

Ernestine Schumann-Heink was very slightly past her prime. If she'd been at the tip-top, I don't think she'd have bothered with a small-potatoes interview, for *The Milwaukee Sentinel*. She was still commanding standing room only at the opera houses, she was still compared to Maria Malibran and Geraldine Farrar. She was a great contralto and she'd sung with Caruso, but she knew, the way every pro does, that she was on the far side of the mountaintop now, even if her fans hadn't found out. She'd perch gracefully, working hard, for another ten years. She sang for the

American war effort during the first war and she sang for Jewish War Relief. (My mother was Jewish, she said. She gave me tenderness.) She sang for twenty-seven thousand people in Balboa Park. She did lose her fortune in the Crash and I read that one of her sons died and she was reduced to evenings of "Danny Boy" and "Silent Night" and shilling baby food but from what I heard, she died a diva, surrounded by unpaid dressers, buckets of roses, and silk sheets.

I was young. I was late. I was soaking wet. Her maid hung my dubious raincoat in a corner. I babbled about Geraldine Farrar's spoiled dog, to show that I was firmly in Madame Schumann-Heink's camp, and I told her I wanted to get a German shepherd. I told her that I pictured a Christmas card of me and the dog in matching raincoats, and in December, in matching Santa hats, and she laughed.

"You are charming," she said. "Rough outside, sweet inside. *Franzbrötchen.*"

The maid gave me a look and poured us glasses of Riesling. A waiter from the hotel brought us a proper German dinner: crisp duck and peeled potatoes sprinkled with parsley, and hot, sharp purple cabbage with caraway seeds and a whipped cream torte. The only one of those things I'd eaten before was potatoes.

It was a long, languorous dinner. (Call me Tini, everyone does.) I'd had fun dinners on boardinghouse floors with cheap bottles of wine and roasted bratwursts and girls who thought I was the next William Allen White or maybe the next Steinbeck or maybe, at least, the next Edna Ferber but I'd never sat on a velvet divan with a famous and perfumed woman kissing my neck, pressing her pearls against my overheated skin, saying, I'm going to loosen my stays, *mausebar.* You pour us another glass.

At midnight, I struggled to my feet.

"Must you?" she said.

"I'm the society editor. I have to be at work early."

"Wonderful. Interviewed by an editor. Come back after."

I came back as soon as I could, and we slept until sunlight came through the crack between the curtains. I could hear the maid in the outer room, piling plates, picking up glasses, talking to herself in German. I was naked. Tini was in layers of lilac silk. She pulled off her eye mask (black silk with a pair of blue velvet eyelids). She kissed me on the shoulder and then on the mouth and she called out for coffee, in German.

The maid came in with a big wooden breakfast tray twice her size, pulled out its little legs, and set it over Tini, as if I wasn't there. She poured from a blue and gold china coffeepot and arranged sugar cubes, and their tongs, and small and large teaspoons, and two dishes of jam, one ringed with blue ceramic flowers and the other with white. There was a basket of muffins, about eight inches high, and a butter dish with a cow on top of it. The cow's tail made the handle. The maid was just on the other side of the bed, picking up Tini's underclothes, pulling at the bed skirt and looking away from me. I squirmed under the sheets, knowing my hair was a mess and my lips were red and my bare shoulders showed. My underpants were on the floor, near the maid's feet. I will go to my grave feeling that I have only just stopped being the hired girl and I wanted this skinny, frowning German woman to know that I was on her side and I was not whatever she thought I was.

Tini spoke sharply in German and the woman left, giving me one long look. Tini hummed and buttered the muffins and put a layer of lemon curd on one half, cut it into pieces, and fed it to me.

"I'm the Marschallin," she said. "You're my Count Octavian."

"I don't know what that is," I said. I worried about the muffin falling on the silk duvet.

She sang a little in German. It was beautiful and very sad.

"Who died?" I said.

She sat up to pour herself another coffee.

"*Der Rosenkavalier.* I'm never going to play this part. It's an exquisite role for a soprano, the Marschallin. She knows that she's going to lose her young lover, sooner or later. And she does. And she sings the hell out of it."

She stood up in her silk layers and put on her robe, rose velvet like the curtains, with thick bands of silk quilting at the hem and cuffs. She pinned up her hair and stretched her neck from side to side. She pulled back her shoulders and lifted her breasts with both hands. She exhaled and closed her eyes and I understood that she was going to perform for me. She opened her mouth and I laughed because I had never heard a person make those sounds and I cried for the odd beauty and whatever it was she was saying goodbye to.

She stood for another minute, the last notes climbing. She held the pose, chin up, hand outstretched to whoever it was that was breaking her heart and then she shrugged. I clapped. I patted the bed and she lay down beside me, a little worse for wear. I poured her a glass of water in the bathroom and she called to me to make it tepid, not cold.

"She leaves the count, because he's too young for her. It's a trousers part. You are my Count Octavian, my beautiful boy, who's really a girl. I used to think Strauss was an idiot about women, but I was wrong."

"I don't think age is such an important thing," I said.

"That's lovely."

We finished the muffins.

"You go in the bathroom and wash up and get dressed, so you don't have to face Berthe. She'll perform her magic and when you come out, I will be presentable and we can take a little walk."

We walked through the park, slowly. I held her parasol and she named the flowers. She commented on what women wore, on the men's hats. (Farmers, she said. There are Bavarians, even here.) We circled back to the hotel for tea and a nap. I ran back to my office for a few hours every day. Tini gave performances every night, for different charities and on the nights I remember, an old man took me down to her dressing room and Berthe let me in. There was a pile of cards, in and out of their envelopes, near her cold cream. There were bouquets wilting in their paper cones and my job was to transfer them to whatever jars and vases and beer bottles Berthe could find. One night, there were two other women in the dressing room, one tall and slim, in a long black dress with a starry ring of diamonds around her neck, and another, in navy-blue silk and pearls, built more along the lines of Tini. Tini gestured to them, and to me. I didn't catch their names. They smiled at me and spoke in German. Tini washed and creamed her face, as if she were alone. She wiped everything off her face until it was just a slab of white flesh, with tired brown eyes. She pulled off her false eyelashes and put them in Berthe's hand. Berthe massaged her neck and shoulders. Tini talked to the women and they laughed and when Berthe came back in with four beers, the tall woman handed me one and winked. I had not been sure what they thought but then she winked and the other one arched her eyebrow and I held on to the beer bottle, embarrassed but not sorry.

We had been together for eleven days. I covered a society luncheon uptown and hurried to her hotel, with a big sheaf of roses and stock. (Carnations are cheap and chrysanthemums are death, she said. No one wants those.) She was dressed the way she was when I met her, in her traveling suit, girded up like a queen, in her wide, gold-buckled belt and a big pearl pin on her lacy lapel. Berthe walked past me with the smallest of the suitcases and a driver came in for the others. I should have asked her not to go, or asked her if I could come with, even though it wouldn't have done any good. I was Milwaukee and already in her rearview mirror, but I wish I had asked, for me. For practice.

"*Schatzie,*" she said. "I can't stay. You'll ruin me."

She kissed me on the cheek.

She took a pretty ring off her finger and put it on my pinkie.

I was crying and looking at the ring on my big hand and still hanging on her sleeve.

"It's a nice little sapphire," she said. "And a couple of diamonds. If you have bad times, you should get a few hundred for it."

"I'm never going to sell this."

"Life is long, *mausebar.*" She kissed me very hard, squeezing my jaw so I opened up to her. She handed the flowers to Berthe and walked out.

Seventeen years later, in love with Eleanor, it was the only pretty and expensive thing I had to give.

Puttin' On the Ritz

. . . .

SUNDAY AT DUSK, APRIL 29, 1945
29 Washington Square West
New York, New York

"I got a very sweet note from your Marion Harron," Eleanor says. "She really is a very sweet person."

"She is," I say. "And a first-rate judge."

"I'm sure she's missing you terribly," Eleanor says.

She doesn't offer to show me the note.

The last time Eleanor and Marion saw each other was almost a year ago. Eleanor had sent a note on White House stationery to Marion and handed one to me over breakfast, inviting us to a White House lunch. Marion propped hers up on her mantel, in her Washington apartment, for anyone who dropped by. I didn't tell her that Eleanor and I had gone back and forth for six months, Eleanor wanting us to come, saying she wanted to give Marion a warm welcome and me resisting, because I didn't want to back a losing horse—I apologize for the phrase—and then there was a turn between me and Marion, the kind you hope for. I'd wake up next to her feeling loved, not smothered, feeling sexy, not cold and

I called out to Eleanor, when I passed her in the White House hall, that Marion and I would really love to join her for lunch. Two weeks went by without a word on the subject. Then, the invitations.

I sat in Marion's living room, so we could drive over to the White House, like we were both visitors. She called me into the bedroom. She wore a blue skirt and a pretty peppermint-striped blouse and a pair of red fuck-me pumps. Yowza, I said. She took them off. She came back in sensible navy walking shoes and I said that even if I was a lesbian lady of a certain age, she was not. She said she thought the walking shoes were appropriate and I said that wearing shoes like Winston Churchill's hand-me-downs was not appropriate for our lunch at the White House.

"You still love her," Marion said.

"Of course I love her," I said. "To know her is to love her. She's an extraordinary person."

Marion said, "I'm a Democrat, I know. I don't mean you admire her. I *admire* her. I mean you're still in love with her."

I said it wasn't true. And it wasn't. I wasn't in love with Eleanor. We had agreed that "in love" had burned out after four years for us, the way it does for most of us, in two months or two years and, I guess, never for some lucky people. Instead of a trail of fire roaring through, those people get small candles steadily lighting the way home until death do they part, and only the young are stupid enough to think that those two old people, him gimping, her squinting, are not in love. I got by. I lived amputated, which sounds worse than it felt. I learned to do all kinds of large and small tasks, with part of me missing, and I feel pretty sure that the people who watched me in the world thought that I was entirely able-bodied. (Often broke, occasionally bitter, but not disabled.)

"I want you all to myself," Marion said.

"You have me," I said. Which is why, although I talk plenty of trash about Franklin, I have never faulted him for telling women what they want to hear.

Every couple has the same five arguments in their lifetime, which is really just the one, over and over, until people die or divorce. What it is depends on who you are and what your parents did to you. Franklin said, Love me, without criticism or condition, and Eleanor said, Be worthy of my love. Or maybe Eleanor said, Make life matter, and Franklin said, Make life easy.

With Ellie, my first girlfriend, rich, pretty, and a bottomless well, our only argument was her saying to me, You don't love me, and me arguing that I did. I said I loved her deeply and truly. I said that anyone with eyes could see how much I loved her but that it was my nature to be a little reticent, to grumble, to keep my softer emotions in check.

We broke up and stayed friends of a certain kind (the kind where the person you've hurt gets happily married and comes to see you as a dodged bullet). We never argued again. And I'd found myself having that same argument twenty years later with Marion, who was twice as smart as Ellie and probably loved me twice as much, from which I conclude that the problem is not the women in my life.

"You're gorgeous," I said. "Please put on the red shoes, and take off your skirt."

I made love to her as if we had twenty minutes to live and we were a little late to lunch and both of us were flushed and all of that was okay with me.

We passed the guards, the Secret Service, two aides, a couple of maids, and Tommie Thompson, and every one of them lit up, as if Marion Harron was a favorite niece come to visit. At last, they could just like me, or not. I wasn't the worm in the apple, anymore. I was just a plain old visiting apple, and nobody minds that.

"Iced tea, hot tea, or sherry," Eleanor said.

Marion declared that she loved tea. I asked for sherry. I thought lunch couldn't last more than an hour and voilà, we'd already used up four minutes on beverage choice.

Marion thought lunch was an invitation to confide in Eleanor. She talked about how well I'd done with my diabetes, about my admirable willpower, about the peonies she planted at my house on Long Island. She talked a little bit about her admiration for both Roosevelts, about her own dear mother and how hard it had been to move out of her family home, and finally, get settled in a place of her own ("soon to be our own," she said). She talked about her thesis in law school on Justice Louis Brandeis and how much she'd learned from me about writing a clear sentence.

"You know how Lorena is," Marion said. "So direct. Such a strong, smart writer, and no depth or important detail is ever sacrificed. She goes after my baggy sentences, all my convolutions, and she just blows them apart, like a strong sea breeze."

Eleanor nodded and smiled. "Oh yes," she said.

We ate the terrible food.

I talked about my new job with the Democratic National Committee, and I told a funny story about me and Gladys Tillett giving a speech and knocking them dead in a hick town, until the audience realized we weren't from the DAR. Marion said that I was a fierce advocate and Eleanor smiled. Eleanor mentioned she'd been in Puerto Rico and she said that she'd thought about our time there ten years ago.

"It ended up being a huge press junket," Eleanor said. "The kind I get in trouble for now."

I said that it hadn't started out that way, that it had just been me and Eleanor going to do some investigation for Federal Relief. We'd seen ourselves as partners, and pioneers.

Eleanor said, "Well, it ended up being a big group, didn't it?"

I said that it had been a fucking circus and we both shut up.

Eleanor called for dessert and talked about where her sons were stationed and her constant worry about them. Marion made sympathetic noises. Eleanor held forth about wartime economies and sugar rationing and the kind of recipes she recommended, which was hilarious, all things considered.

I asked if the prune whip in front of us was one of the new recipes.

It was, she said.

I said I thought it might be and we looked each other in the eye.

Eleanor said that it was a shame, but we had to end our luncheon. She said that she hoped we'd have a chance to do this again soon.

"With Lorena still living here, you'll get tired of seeing me," Marion said.

Eleanor said that it was wonderful to be able to host me for a little while longer. I said I appreciated it. Eleanor said she was glad I had no complaints and Marion said that honestly she'd never heard me complain and Eleanor raised an eyebrow. Everyone kissed everyone goodbye.

When I moved out of the White House, I moved into Marion's new apartment and Eleanor sent a big silver vase. I left it on the mantel when I moved out.

"You broke her heart," Eleanor says to me.

I don't say a word.

...

Eleanor didn't keep secrets from me. If transparency is a sign of true love, then I was loved, like nobody's business. She told me all of her ups and downs, the deepest depressions, even her complete and sweet delight when one more person, great or small, adored her. And she liked to hear about everything in my life that needed fixing or saving, wise counsel or sympathy, and I told her plenty: unpaid bills, unappreciative bosses, the occasional diabetic coma, and some other colossal errors in judgment. I loved being the brave and battered little dinghy. She loved being the lighthouse. It worked for both of us, perfectly for four years, and imperfectly since then, and what I've kept to myself is only what she doesn't really want to know.

My friendship with Parker Fiske was one of those things. We saw each other at the Rowers Inn, where I ran a tab, and at a race-track dive in Baltimore, where he did.

I even met with him at his house in Maryland. His chauffeur drove me through antique wrought-iron gates about eighteen feet high and down a mile-long gravel drive. We drove past horses and even a few painterly cows, grazing among the trees and the honeysuckle. Jonquils and buttercups were thick on the ground, tossed all over the green lawn, like handfuls of gold. I'd been to the Big House in Hyde Park plenty, and six governors' houses, and a few movie stars', and I had lived in the White House. Hyde Park was just an old country home, stuffed with heirlooms and crap by a woman whose terrible taste was formed in the 1880s. The White House, my home away from home and the seat of power in the Western world notwithstanding, was just a rambling, run-down boardinghouse for the extended Roosevelt family. White Horse Hill Manor was beauty itself, shaped like a house.

There wasn't a butler. Parker Fiske took my hat and coat in the big front hall. Now, may I call you Hick? he said. You call me Parker.

He looked thinner and older. He had dark blue circles under his eyes. There were faded murals of Greek gods (I think; I saw a swan with a coy look) on one of the walls and worn Oriental rugs over squares of black-and-white marble. Eleanor had taught me about vulgar, and I was pretty sure this wasn't vulgar. I'd never been in a place that so impressed me and I tried to shake it off.

He led me into the kitchen.

"I'll make us some lunch," he said. "I love scrambling eggs. Eleanor and I are as one in our domestic inclinations. Good on a little light nourishment, useless otherwise. I'm the one who should be famous for wheeling in a bar cart with all the fixings and whipping up eggs, every time Cousin Franklin wins an election. I love cracking the eggs"—he did it one-handed in a big white bowl and looked to see that I'd noticed—"making that splash. The whisking. Eleanor can't actually cook, you know. Of course you know. Did you leave her a little note that we were lunching today?"

I had not.

He poured the eggs in.

"I go low and slow, the way eggs should be cooked. Also, entre nous, a little hot sauce."

He wiped one hand on the gray canvas apron covering his trousers and elegant white shirt, and tied in front, like a real chef. He added chives and diced red pepper and shreds of yellow cheese, from small, pretty ceramic bowls. He pinched salt into his palm and tossed it in. His pepper grinder was the size of a lamp and he tossed it from hand to hand and made a few turns with it. He put four slices of toast (Brioche, he said. Melts in your mouth, and isn't that what we want?) in an old-fashioned toaster, which brought the slices so close to the red-hot coils, they smoked. He spooned eggs onto my plate. I was eating scrambled eggs and buttering toast with a man I liked, who seemed to mean me harm.

"Let's not talk business over lunch. In re Eleanor's cooking, it's too bad you missed their wedding. One of the highlights of my life. The food was terrible. She looked beautiful."

I smiled. It was my favorite thing to hear.

"Oh, you do love her. That wedding was quite a do. The food, well, I said. Have you ever been to a Jewish wedding? I love Jews. The Roosevelt wedding was the opposite. Enough booze to float the Navy, as it were, and barely enough stale sandwiches for the first hundred guests. Potted shrimp. Cucumber disks with a wisp of crème fraîche, a hint, really, and exactly one tiny, tiny caviar egg. People think he was so dashing back then, not that *you'd* make that mistake. He was a stuffed shirt and a bit awkward and when he was at Harvard I don't think there were five men outside the family who liked him. Everyone *loved* Eleanor. Not Cousin Alice but Alice was a bitch, even then. Talk about See You Next Tuesday. Oh, I see we are in complete agreement, Miss Hick. Alice was *jealous*. Teddy never loved her. You know he would have thrown Alice in a ditch to have had Eleanor as his own, natural child. Plenty of young men, believe me, admired that beautiful pile of hair and her big beautiful blue eyes. And her brains. And her posture. Eleanor Roosevelt knows how to cross a room. One could marry Eleanor with full confidence that she'd never make a scene or throw a bowl, or do something ridiculous in public. Well, not quite, as it turns out."

He buttered more toast. He poured himself a coffee cup of Scotch and waved the bottle at me. I shook my head but I liked his style. I missed my tough and reckless friends, rounding the corners too hard.

"Aren't you wise?"

I ate like I was alone, eyes down and steady. I peppered my eggs. I sipped the excellent Bloody Mary he put in front of me. He put his hand on my shoulder.

"Whitman said, 'I am as bad as the worst but, thank God, I am as good as the best.' You ought to spend more time with people who know how bad they are."

"Well, I know," I said.

"Good. You know. I know. Forgive me for beating this particular horse, but people are going to find out about the two of you," he said.

"They will if you have your way," I said. "This is the best Bloody Mary I've ever had."

He grinned like a boy. "Celery salt. Bring your drink and let's sit in the drawing room. It is beautiful in there today. The light. Like a Bonnard."

He put out his hand for mine and led me into the beautiful pine-paneled library.

"You're literary," he said. "I thought you'd like this."

"I'm not literary," I said.

The pillows on the divan were rough blue silk, with thick, softly twisted blue and gold fringe. I wanted to lie down among them.

"No? Aren't you the writer? Half of Washington thinks you ghostwrite everything she does. The My Day columns, and let me just say, my God, who can churn that out six days a week? The books. *This Is My Story, This Troubled World, This Merry Christmas.* Whathaveyou. More coming, I'm sure."

"I'm sure," I said. I was sure. Eleanor loved to write in a way that is not natural for writers. She ripped off sentences like unspooling a thread. She wrote letters to all of her loved ones, not only because she loved us, but because she loved the pen racing across the paper. She loved the appearance of her thoughts in blue ink on white paper. She could have had a bake-off with Anthony Trollope and come in first, most of the time.

"She must keep you busy, writing in the shadows."

"I'm not. I write for money, I always have. I'm not her ghost-writer. She loves to write. I'm a journalist, an ink-stained wretch. I stand with Samuel Johnson."

He waved his glass at me.

"'No man but a blockhead ever wrote, except for money.' I had no idea you were so . . . erudite."

"Or even educated."

"As you say. It can't be easy, making your living as any kind of writer, knowing that everyone who hires you is, in some way, waiting for the big White House scoop. Or wanting to please Eleanor. I mean, you're talented, I remember those Lindbergh articles. It's not really fair."

It wasn't fair to me, it had not been fair for the last ten years, and even when Eleanor did leave the White House, I didn't see my career taking a terrific upturn. Parker Fiske was the only person in the world who'd ever said so. Everyone else said I was lucky.

"Why am I here?" I said.

"Why did you come?"

I said that I'd come because he sent a car and a driver. I said my curiosity would probably be the death of me and that I hoped he hadn't poisoned the eggs.

"I have no wish to poison you," he said. "I wish to help you, and the woman you love. And I wish for you to help me. You see, utterly transparent."

"I don't think I can help you, Mr. Fiske."

"Parker, please. Well, let's talk about you first. I know you don't want people gossiping about you and Eleanor."

"I don't care if people talk," I said. "Eleanor and I are very good, very dear friends."

I was anxious and my voice rose. I sounded a little like Eleanor.

"Yes, I heard you'd moved on. That pretty judge. Harmon? Harron? Of course you care. Eleanor doesn't care because she doesn't have to. She's been in gold armor her whole life. She cares about the suffering of the poor, which is completely to her credit, but you actually know what the suffering of the poor is like. She doesn't. And what has her suffering been, in fact? A foolish and unkind mama and Franklin's harem but, on the other hand, First Lady. It may bother her, more than she lets on, that there are people who don't like her pushy, Negro-loving, Bolshevik ways. I do, by the way."

"Me too," I said.

I lifted my glass in a way that said, Let's have another, and he poured more Bloody Mary from a tall, almost frosted silver pitcher. He pulled a celery stalk from a crystal snifter, gave it a shake to open the leaves, and put that in my glass too.

"There is going to be a big, juicy, headline-shredding scandal in the White House coming up and unless we do something about it, it will probably destroy the President's reputation and his legacy," he said.

"We? It won't be about me and Eleanor," I said. "It's over. We're as dull as rocking chairs. Just like you said, it's me and the judge these days."

"Dull's in the eye of the beholder. And the point's not to catch you between the sheets. Not anymore. The point is, you were the First Lady's lesbian lover. The point is, she had a lover. The point is, you're a lesbian."

I said I was following him so far. I said we'd already been through this the last time, in the diner, and I thought he'd let it go.

"I'm sorry about that. I was already running scared and I thought you'd be useful, if you were scared too. I thought we might share information. I didn't even have a proper plan. I suppose I thought that I would wave scandal at you and you'd leak me useful tidbits and I'd pass them on to J. Edgar Hoover and he'd keep my files to himself. But, you weren't scared enough," he said. "You were too goddamn happy. Afterward, I thought about you. I liked the cut of your jib. How's that?"

"Hilarious," I said. "I'm still happy. It must be my nature."

"Like mine."

We both laughed.

"I don't even have tidbits for you, these days," I said. "The Roosevelt sons are not paragons of virtue. Anna loves her father. Princess Martha of Norway is just as good-looking in person, lusting for Franklin, and a goddamn idiot. Does that help?"

He smiled. He stood up and paced.

"You're not making this easy. Very soon, I'm going to be at the center of a hideous scandal. All sorts of virtuous nonsense in bold type, about my perverse predilections. I'll have to resign. Franklin will have to accept my resignation. You know how it is. You can raise your baby as your sister, knock up the housemaid and deny your own son, lie to your sterile husband about your bouncing baby boy, bring smallpox to the New World and sell opium from sea to sea, but . . ."

I said I agreed with him. I liked his patter. I even liked our lunch and I forgave him, even while he was threatening me. I hadn't had a pal like him in years. In the White House, we did good and we talked nice.

"I am making a terrible mess of this," he said. "Let me try again: Wouldn't it be something if the scandal that pushes mine off the front page is you and Eleanor, with a nasty quote from Cousin Alice, and maybe some photos of your little judge, just to show that not only are you Eleanor's lesbian lover, but you are a serpent of unnatural desire, spreading your poison everywhere. You know. And if your story gets rolled out right away, and I think I can manage that, the lesbian rumpus will overshadow mine entirely. I mean, I'm an underling. Eleanor is First Lady. You see."

He said this all in the most cheerful, instructive way, like a friendly schoolteacher.

I finished my drink and stood up. He took my hand.

"That's the worse-case scenario, as Mr. Hoover likes to put it. And I'm sorry to even bring it up. But if you help me," he said, "if you and Eleanor could get Franklin to stand by me, no one has to suffer. No stories of any kind. You see? What I want is that none of us suffer. Even J. Edgar is not inclined to put his big Mary Jane into it."

Twenty years ago, I would have broken some dishes and blacked his eye. Even now, it was no trouble to stand up to him and say, Don't pull this blackmail bullshit on me, buster, but I didn't see the reason for it. He was neck-deep in trouble and reaching for the nearest branch. It could have been me begging him for help, if it had all gone the other way. Eleanor'd known Parker Fiske since he was born. She'd stand by him and she'd tell Franklin to stand by him. And Franklin would want to. It'd be good, clean fun for him, thwarting the State Department. And there was no reason for me not to back Parker Fiske and no one cared, really, what I did. It was flattering that Parker didn't seem to grasp that.

"All right," I said. "No suffering. There's enough. Eleanor and Franklin will back you. One hundred percent. I'm sure of it. And me. We all will."

He smiled and exhaled.

"And, please, don't tell her I asked you, unless you must. She wouldn't like it. Just work your magic. Emphasize the good I have done. Next time," he said, "you girls come out together and there'll be a beautiful lunch and we'll spend a lovely afternoon."

I said that he might change his ways, going forward, and he smiled tightly. Like you, he said. I said that frankly, I'd been exactly who I was since I was fourteen only now I dressed a little better and kept my temper.

"Well, I have always dressed impeccably," he said. "She's the love of your life, I gather."

I smiled. "She seems to be."

"And are you hers?" he said.

"Close enough," I said.

He leaned toward me.

"Really, Hick," he said. "We could be friends. Of a kind."

"We can," I said.

He raised his elegant hand and the car rolled forward and the chauffeur came out to open the door for me, tipping his hat.

I went to Eleanor about Parker Fiske, without saying anything about the scrambled eggs or White Horse Hill. I said I admired his devotion to this country and that he was a great public servant. She looked at me and said he certainly was. She backed him. Franklin backed him. Even J. Edgar Hoover, in his odd, weaselly way, backed Parker Fiske, and he had read the files and the files, Franklin said, were scorching. And then the Republican senators piled on and Hoover changed his mind and smart money said that Parker Fiske was on his way out. Franklin wrestled and argued and swore that he would kill the secretary of state before he'd lose Parker Fiske (he said that he'd rather be in hell with Parker than in heaven with Republicans). Franklin said just what you'd want your boss to say, up and down the Eastern Seaboard, and then he made himself a martini and accepted Parker's resignation. Too many incidents, Franklin said, for too many years, in too many countries. Too many reports, read by too many enemies. I read the speech Parker gave at Harvard, after he resigned, and it was a barn burner. Eleanor would have been proud to give it. Parker said all people, of all colors, had inalienable human rights and that all colonial rule represented a moral wrong. Franklin never mentioned it.

Eleanor told me she'd written to Parker and Cybele, inviting them to dinner in New York sometime, but she did say she had a lot of other people to see. She saw young people, she saw veterans. She saw socialists. She saw sharecroppers. She walked picket lines and gave her speaking fees to the International Garment Workers. She was famous for going everywhere and seeing everyone, from the soldiers to the coal miners, to the women working lines at the factories. She was ridiculed for caring and she doubled down. She joined the NAACP when white people didn't and she stared down Bull Connor in Birmingham and said that few things had given her as much satisfaction. In this war, our world was changing and people were frightened and they were angry. For every woman working in a factory, thrilled to have a decent job, there were ten men cursing her and another ten making sure that none of the people whom Hitler failed to murder would wind up on our shores, eating at our table. She never stopped. She never read her own press. She never forgot anyone's birthday and she never left anyone off the Christmas list and it was the giving that was the real pleasure, even when the relationship was not what it was. (See: me.) She didn't talk to women about leading by their fine moral example anymore. She didn't talk to anyone about quiet virtue anymore. She went wherever she was invited, and some places she wasn't, and she talked until she was hoarse about the basic rights of every citizen: equal education, equal pay, equal representation, and equal participation. Everyone quoted her and lots of people hated her, and when she said she didn't mind anymore, that she was honored to have an FBI file the size of the Manhattan phone book, she meant it. A lot of Republicans preferred Adolf Hitler to Eleanor Roosevelt, and not because they'd heard that Eleanor and I were lovers ten years ago.

I felt bad for Parker and for the country and I sent him a note, saying so, expressing my admiration and saying his resignation was a loss for the country.

He wrote back.

My dear Hick,
It was very kind of you to write and I hope it has cost you
nothing. My friendship has been so difficult, for so many. I
spend my days with new friends, the fly fishermen of Maine,
and it has been the rest cure everyone said it would be.

My wife has been a great support and never complains. She
has made a very large scrapbook of my positive "press," since my
resignation. I no longer have to wonder what my funeral will
be like.

I'll be returning to White Horse Hill soon. Although I won't
pretend our paths are likely to cross, I hope you know that I will
be delighted if they do.

With kindest regards,
Parker Fiske

No one ever wrote a story about Eleanor and me.

Between You and Me

....

Very early Monday morning, April 30, 1945
29 Washington Square West
New York, New York

It's two A.M. The streetlamp cuts through the curtains. We sleep under a shelf of Roosevelt family photographs. All of the children, her handsome, fraying father, her brother Hall when he was beautiful, Franklin and Eleanor laughing on the lawn, giddy and young.

The last time I saw Franklin, it was two months ago and I was still sleeping in the White House. I'd gone looking for a pen. The ones in my room were dry or broken. Eleanor was asleep and mostly long gone from me. Sometimes, we'd breakfast together and gossip over a stack of newspapers like an old, married couple or we'd spend the afternoon with Tommie typing and Eleanor dictating, just in case I could lend a hand, and once I came upon her crying a little, after a run-in with Franklin Junior, but mostly, we were fond and distant ships passing on the second floor of the White House. I had a very small bedroom and my photograph wasn't on Eleanor's mantel anymore but I had my meals, and very few bills, and I had Marion. I still liked prowling the halls late at night. No one but the Secret Service was around. They nodded, I nodded. I'd go into the kitchen, hoping to find a muffin, then I'd walk back upstairs and look for a pen. When you are waiting for the sun to rise, for the world to join you, any activity seems promising. I walked through the second floor, past all the closed doors, and took the stairs back down.

Franklin was asleep in his wheelchair, head back against the wood frame.

I'd caught him like that once before, years ago, in his first term, with Missy sitting on the couch next to him, in her pink wool robe, holding his hand. She'd seen me and coughed. He opened his tired eyes and waved a hand.

"Well, look here. Hick, couldn't sleep? Come to join the insomniacs club?"

"I guess so. I was looking for a pen, but if you two are having a nightcap, I wouldn't mind."

Missy pursed her lips and shook her head. He grinned. I was still a fresh face. I was an interesting adversary, I knew some good jokes and I could hold my liquor. It was a third-act twist to have drinks with Missy, showing me that he had his woman and he'd also had mine and plenty of minor tail in between. And, he was running the United States, like his very own fiefdom. And, oh, this chair, this minor impediment, nothing to it. I stood my ground. Missy held on to his hand.

"Oh no," she said. "F.D., it's so late."

I don't think people can help it. We play with fire and tell ourselves we're just lighting a modest, necessary candle. We know discretion is called for and everything in us cries out to be seen, to spread our feathers. You're in a bar on West Nineteenth Street, filled with Italians and romantic tourists, and you put your hand over hers, in an unmistakable way, right between the martini glass and the antipasto and you don't move it until the waiter comes and clears his throat to announce the specials. You're at a gathering of people, who are not your friends, and no one has twigged about the two of you and you hear yourself call her Darling, in front of a roomful. I was not someone Missy should have showed off to. I was a pervert. I was madly in love with Eleanor, which I didn't have the decency to hide, being a pervert, and Eleanor seemed to be crazy in love with me, which baffled everyone, since everyone knew passion and romance—and perversion—were not Eleanor Roosevelt's cup of tea. And I'd only just stopped being a reporter. If things went south with Eleanor, who knows what terrible story I might sell to the *Enquirer*. Missy knew all that. And still, she danced her fingers along his arm, up to his broad shoulder. She leaned so close her breast grazed his chest and still leaning in, she kissed him, closer to the lips than the cheek. He patted her hand.

She stood up and straightened her robe. She wanted me to walk out with her. I sat down on the arm of the old leather chair across from Franklin.

"Mr. President," I said. "Missy needs her beauty sleep. You know I don't."

He laughed.

"My dear," he said to her. "Hick'll keep me company for a little while."

She stood in the doorway, grinding her teeth.

"Really, my dear," he said. "Good night."

Oh, I knew that voice. Light and charming and the sun would set on you before you'd even reached the door. And in the face of Franklin's deep freeze, everyone backed down. I sulked. I pretended it was a dignified retreat but it was just lumbering backward, in shame. A few times, when there'd been too much Scotch going around, shame propelled me forward instead, until I was out of my chair, facing him down, with nothing to say. I stood over him, furious with both of us, opening and closing my fists.

He puffed on a cigarette and his eyes wandered from my face to my bosom and back, assessing out of habit, just letting me know. I sat back down and pretended to read. Franklin called for another round. I couldn't scold the President of the United States, whom I admired with all my heart, and I didn't have it in me to fight with the cripple I was cuckolding every night I had the chance.

We sat in the near dark, that first night. All I could see was his silver hair, the steel rims of his glasses, his snowy white cuffs, and his elegant hands.

"Well," he said. "Pour us something."

I poured us what I could find without turning on a light.

"This feels like rum. I found some lime slices," I said.

"Oh, like we're in Cuba," he said. *"Salud."*

"I hope we shall drink down all unkindness," I said. I hoped he'd ask me what that was from and I would say *The Merry Wives of Windsor* and he'd express admiration and surprise. He lifted his glass to me and took a long swallow.

"You're on the road a lot," he said. "Making a point?"

"That Harry Hopkins is a demanding fella."

"Sure. You're a very good reporter," he said, and I was so pleased I blushed.

"So, you're not making a point."

I was making a point. Eleanor was impossible: She'd make and break dates and weep to me because John or Elliott or Anna needed her just when we were supposed to be together. I'd say, Let's just take one day off, go to the Mayflower and stay in bed and she'd act like I was stealing the silver.

I spent the next four months traveling for work, making my point. My letters to her were straight out of the Sapphic Guide to

Summer Travel. Gorgeous weather! Magnificent sunsets! My car's running like a top and did I mention my rekindled friendship with darling Alicent Holt, my former teacher? Why, she's just a little older than you, Dearest, sitting right beside me in the passenger seat, one hand on my knee or a little higher. She loves Emily Dickinson too. There are more charming guesthouses in Michigan, run by more charming spinsters, than you'd guess. I described the pretty rooms, and the heirloom comforters for the still cool nights and in the course of describing the pretty room, I indicated that there was only one comforter and only one bed. As with all good prose, it's not just what you say, it's how you say it. I made it clear that the only thing wrong with Alicent was the way she was, honestly, wearing me out. And at the end of the summer, I'd picked up the thread with dear Lottie, my schoolgirl pal, from South Dakota. (A good reporter can find anyone.) Lottie had raised her kids and after three bad years, her husband was just getting on his feet and if you don't think my bringing a small ham, a bag of oranges, and a bottle of moonshine made me entirely welcome at Lottie's house, you don't know what hard times are like. Was Henry smacking me on the back after a few drinks? Yes, he was. Was Lottie glad to grab a small bag, her skivvies, and cold cream, and drive across the Dakotas and into Iowa, just for old times' sake? Yes, she was and she did and didn't we have fun, in the car and out of it. And, as it always was, she felt that no harm had been done to Henry or her marriage because we were just girls. There was, as Lottie put it, no thing.

"Well, Mr. President . . ." I wondered what I was going to say.

"Never mind. She hasn't been herself."

I brought the bottle to his glass and he shook his head.

"Call Wyatt," he said.

His Secret Service man came in from the hall and Franklin lifted his chin.

"Good night, Miss Hickok. Good to see you again."

Wyatt nodded to me and wheeled Franklin out and to his bedroom. He'd undress the President and put him in pajamas, one thin, useless leg at a time, and Franklin'd slide himself from the chair to the bed, with Wyatt hovering. Wyatt, Secret Service through and through, made sure that the whole procedure was as businesslike as possible. I'd seen it a few times, the transition from the car up the stairs, Franklin carried like a tired child by a big man. It was impossible to find an elegant position. It was impossible for him to be anything but powerless and, because of that, foolish. When he was carried, all of his women looked away.

They loved him. History should show him to be a great man, a great leader, a silver-tongued con man and a devil with women, but if it doesn't show that they adored him, it's not telling the truth. They loved him not despite being a cripple but for it. Before the polio, once he'd made himself assistant secretary to the Navy, women fell for the big smile, the flashing teeth against his beautiful tan, the dimple, the arrogant, defiant chin, the strong thrust of Roosevelt drive but I don't think there's a woman on earth who doesn't like it when a big, strong man is brought a little low. Need is like a handful of salt on the fire for most of us. He was a hell of a man before the polio. Polio made him irresistible.

I'd come back to the White House and found a note on my bed, suggesting we have dinner the next night, "if I wasn't too tired." *I am goddamn exhausted*, I wrote on the back of the note, *but I'll be very happy to have dinner and afterward.*

I slipped the note under her door then and thought, *Salud*.

. . .

Six weeks ago, right before I packed up all my things one more time and thanked the kitchen staff and Mabel who ironed my skirts, I went for my last late-night wander to say goodbye to Franklin, if I saw him. Once I left the White House, our paths wouldn't cross. Eleanor was visiting an airplane factory. Missy was dead and buried in Massachusetts. Princess Martha, who'd refused to take a hint, had stayed on weeks after the fourth inauguration and had finally taken her pretty, relentless self back to Norway to look after Cosmo and Cuckoo, or whatever her children were called.

It seemed that we were winning the war. It seemed that the end was coming soon, and that it was going our way. We still had blackout curtains on every window, and some of the biggest windows were painted black. Black paint spattered the carpet edges in every big room. At night, the streets were empty and quiet and the streetlights near us stayed dark all night. There were gun crews on the roof and the food was even worse than before, because Eleanor insisted that the White House suffer rationing, like everyone else. One week, we didn't have eggs. We had oily dabs of yellow and white margarine on whole wheat toast and found it as disgusting as everyone else. Whatever the kitchen was calling hamburger, the President didn't eat it and neither did I and neither did the dog. White House coffee was always weak and now it was a little worse, and in smaller cups. Eleanor didn't allow complaining. She pointed out that all the other countries at war were truly suffering from privation. She flashed Franklin's war rations coupon book whenever she could, fanning the pages out and saying, with real regret, Ours is such a small sacrifice. But the small, constant waves of anxiety had worn us out. People walked into meetings, said what they had to say, and slammed out. I passed old men outside Franklin's office with their faces to the wall, crying. Jewish men and women came in, in furs or nearly in rags, carrying babies or with their rabbis, with their most important people and they left, in fury and despair. Two men in black hats and long coats prayed in the hall. Every Jewish friend the Roosevelts had begged Franklin to do more, sooner, and got nowhere. Elinor Morgenthau came in her furs and flowers and her Lilly Daché hat to hold hands with Eleanor. She walked out two hours later, ten years older. Negro men in uniform came to the office, three at a time. I heard some laughter and then low voices and the Negro men walked out, standing tall, eyes straight ahead. People smoked everywhere. There were overflowing ashtrays and buckets of sand in case of fire, side by side, in every room.

The war had made the inauguration short and simple and even so it was too much for us. Eleanor corralled all thirteen grandchildren and every dreadful cousin. His address lasted five minutes, which might be the shortest ever. It was bitter cold for Washington and we had snow. Franklin didn't wear his hat or coat and no one said he should. He looked like hell. A thousand people came to the White House that day and Eleanor received every single person on the line. Franklin ate in the back, with some of his harem, and rested. People came in to praise him, to beg for favors, to mention their own hopes and wishes, and on the way out, every single one of those people informed Eleanor that maybe she didn't realize this, but she should ask less of him and take better care of him. She knew he was dying of something and he knew he was dying. He chose this, is what they both thought and by God, he was going out as the greatest president this country ever knew and not as some fading invalid who couldn't remember where Yugoslavia was or why it mattered. Louis Howe was dead. Sara Delano Roosevelt was dead, which was terrible for Franklin. Hall Roosevelt died a few weeks later, grieving and relieving the family. Harry Hopkins was out of the White House and near dead himself. Two old friends had died at the end of February and now there was almost no one for Franklin to lean on.

The light was on in his office and the door was open. I knocked.

"Looking for a pen?" he said.

"People walk off with them. After the inauguration, I saw all kinds of things disappear. You're lucky the dog's still here."

He patted Fala's ears.

"I hear you've still got your place on Long Island."

"On my way. I'm retiring there," I said. "It's my Warm Springs, my Little White House. I'll be there when the forsythia come out."

He put his head back and rested it.

"The places we love. The people we love."

We sat there for a long time.

"You and the missus, the fire's gone out?"

I exhaled. If we were playing Honesty, I was not going to lose to a man who lied with every breath.

"We love each other. I would do anything for her and I feel lucky, I feel honored, to be her dear friend."

"That little judge of yours. Marion Harron. Hot ticket."

Thank you didn't seem like the right answer.

"Fires go out," he said. "We know that. All fires go out, goddamnit."

"Yes, sir."

"Oh, for God's sake, Hick."

"Yes, sir, all fires go out. It doesn't mean that we don't still want to sit by the fireplace, I guess."

"Fair point," he said. "I'm going to Warm Springs, as a matter of fact, in a couple of weeks. To sit by the fireplace. Get a little rest. Encourage the other polios."

"Then don't bring Cousin Polly. Jingle jangle."

He laughed.

"Well, she's colorful. And Daisy will come. Don't bother saying something nice, I know you think she's an idiot. A couple of friends might stop by. A painter lady. Going to do my portrait."

"That'll be handsome."

I hoped it would be handsome. If she painted him as he was now, he'd look ancient and worried and not long for this world. His full, handsome face was wolfhound thin now and he looked like nothing so much as an aristocratic Jesus, hanging off the cross.

"When the time comes, you're the one she should be with. You're the one she should be rocking on the porch with."

"Like she'll be rocking on the porch."

He laughed again, as light as paper turning.

"If she's rocking on a porch, I think it'll be with Joe Lash and Trude, and little baby Lash," I said.

"You're wrong. That's their life, that's not hers. He'll get plenty out of her, I know, but sitting with the Lashes is not going to be her life. If she runs for office, that's too bad for you," he said, coolly. "But, you could write her speeches."

"She's very fond of Joe," I said, poking him a little.

He snorted. "There'll be others. More sons. That's not the point. You're the one. Don't give up on her," he said. "Don't be so proud."

"Okay," I said.

We sat together until he fell asleep in the chair and I left the room, telling the new Secret Service man he was resting.

Parting

· ·

Someone's banging on the door. I reach for Eleanor.
"Stay here," I say.

She reaches for her robe.

"Eleanor, goddamnit, stay here."

We are both still half-asleep, looking for our glasses, stumbling in the dark room. I kiss her on the forehead and press her to lie down. Just don't move, I say. She squeezes my hand and says, Dearest.

I pick up the bread knife and move down the hall. A man calls out, Mrs. Roosevelt, and I open the door. A dark-skinned Negro man is cradling a tall white man in his arms, on the floor. He says he is very sorry for troubling us and the man in his arms groans again and I see that the Negro man is beautiful and wearing glasses. There is a bright, narrow slash of blood across his high forehead. His tweed sports jacket is ripped down the back.

The white man's face is a bloody mask. The blood has mostly come down over his eyes from a gash in his scalp at the crown. His left ear is crumpled and bleeding at the top and his whole face is like a piece of raw beef. He is crying, I think. His mouth opens and closes, showing his bloody teeth. I was a reporter for a long time and I recognize his English shoes.

"Parker," I say.

"Hick."

The other man, holding Parker Fiske, like he is the mother and Fiske a fallen soldier, says "Thurman Jones, ma'am."

Eleanor comes out in her wrapper and both men get to their feet.

I tell them, Come on in. I tell Eleanor to please get some brandy or Scotch and I'll get the towels. We sit in a heap on the living room floor and while Thurman Jones holds Parker's head, I blot up the blood with a warm washcloth and two of Eleanor's monogrammed hand towels. Parker's face emerges. I see the long, sharp nose and his owlish eyes. He puts his hand up to see if the blood has stopped and takes out his spectacles. His white shirt is dark red except at the cuffs.

"Oh my," he says. "Look where we have found ourselves, Thurman. A love nest. I thought it would just be you, Eleanor."

Eleanor kneels next to Parker. She does a good job with a couple of butterfly bandages. She always travels with a first aid kit the size of a hatbox and I used to tell her that she would have been happiest as a nurse.

Parker says, "I'm not drunk."

Thurman Jones shakes his head. "Not now."

"You know that song," Parker says. He sits up slowly, leaning on the black man's shoulder, and he lifts both his hands, with imaginary maracas. *We'll find a little hideaway, where we can hide away the time. We'll stay away, with lemon and lime.*"

They sit down on the couch, knees touching. I ask Thurman Jones what he'd like to drink and he says he would really like a cup of tea, if it's not too much trouble. You know that line from Pinero's play, he adds, "While there is tea, there is hope." Eleanor smiles and hops up. She already likes him so much more than Cousin Parker.

It would be all right with Eleanor if Parker doesn't tell us a thing. It would be ideal if he could maintain a Rooseveltian silence about the details and leave after a light lunch, patched up and on his way with his charming Negro friend. Parker tells us everything: a downtown club, with a private party in the back, an oil-slicked boy curled up in a giant martini glass, and two girls, in red silk teddies, doing the Carolina Shag. Bricktop was giving the performance of a lifetime, he says. Bricktop. I will never forget it. You'd have lost your mind, Hick.

It sounds wonderful, Eleanor says. Thurman nods.

Cole Porter adores Bricktop, Parker adds. She's opening a club in Mexico City. Speaking of which, that's where we were headed, which is why we have had to come to you in this dreadful condition. I am sorry for the intrusion.

Thurman says, in the most careful, hopeful, worried way, "Cuernavaca. We would go to Paris, but they're all trying to come here. Cuernavaca would be a great place for us. Parker's emptied his accounts. I got an advance on my novel. We have our suitcases in Parker's car."

"A novel," I say. "Well, you're getting plenty of material."

Thurman smiles and I think, Oh my, what is going to happen to you, with my man Parker as your guide.

I mention that Cuernavaca might be pretty rowdy and I happen to have a little place on Long Island, which could be perfect for a novelist. Peace and quiet might be just the ticket, I say.

"It's his second novel," Parker says. "Thurman is a great novelist. He is extraordinary. Countee Cullen said that Thurman's first book was brilliant. Luminous. It was reviewed in *The New York Times*. Mrs. Roosevelt is a wonderful reader, Thurman."

"That's wonderful," Eleanor says. "I must get a copy."

"I'll send you one," Thurman Jones says. "I'll inscribe it."

Eleanor beams.

"We'll buy a bunch," I say. "We'll hand them out like candy canes at Christmastime."

Parker clears his throat.

"The evening didn't end well. Obviously. There were arrests. Thurman and I were arrested for disorderly behavior and other things. We're being arraigned. They have our passports."

"Sons of bitches," I say, and Eleanor purses her lips.

Parker says, like he is explaining to a child how to do arithmetic, "Eleanor, if they have our passports, we can't go to Mexico. If we don't get out of here, we will both be serving time, in prison, for unnatural acts. It's not just disturbing the peace."

"I am so terribly sorry," Eleanor says.

"Eleanor, my dear, we need your help. All you have to do is call La Guardia, he loves you. You were the Assistant Crumbcake of Civil Hoo-Ha, whatever it was. You were magnificent, everyone says so."

"Assistant director for civil defense" I say, and I give him the eye.

"Exactly," Parker says. "Yes. Please. Call the Little Flower, tell him we are not the scum of the earth. We are decent men who got a little carried away and would like nothing more than to leave his fair city immediately, passports in hand, never to return and without corrupting a single moral, anywhere."

Eleanor pours more tea for Thurman. She sighs and stands up.

"Give me a moment, please," she says.

We watch her go. Parker squeezes my hand.

"For Jesus's sake, please, one more time. Speak up for me."

I follow Eleanor into the bedroom. She's in her slip, putting on her plainest dress. I sit on the bed and watch her dress, which I always love to do, knowing each covered part so well, and the look on her face makes me cry.

"I cannot call Fiorello La Guardia and tell him not to clean up his city," she whispers. "There are laws. It is his city. You said to me, there's more life coming. I believe you. You said I can be of use. I believe I can be of use. Perhaps I can make a difference. And I cannot squander the little influence I have. Not for this."

I stand behind her, my arms around her waist, her hand over mine. My chin rests on her shoulder. We see each other in the mirror. She is a little broader now. I am a little less broad. Our eyes meet and she looks away, toward the window. When she came in the door Friday night, she wore grief upon fatigue upon disappointment at what the future would not bring and beneath that, a stab of relief at knowing. I look like that now.

"Not for this?" I say. "Should we be in jail? We like to hold hands when the lights are low. Even now. You can make the call, darling. This is exactly your kind of call. Parker was a great servant to this country. Thurman is a great novelist. I think they love each other."

"I'm sure they do," she says. She shakes her head and goes back into the living room. I make myself follow her.

She tells Parker that she is very sorry but she cannot do anything for him, that she is nothing more than a great man's widow, that she has no influence at all, in this kind of thing.

Parker and Thurman stand up.

I tell them that they should leave town anyway. There's a war on, I say. Even Fiorello La Guardia is not going to send New York City police officers all the way to the West Coast to track down a couple of deviants. I smile when I say deviants and Thurman gives me the thumbs-up. Parker and Eleanor are like stone. You hide out in Los Angeles for a while, I say, and sooner than you can say Cary Grant, you'll get a few fancy friends to pull some strings and you can just slip into Cuernavaca. It can't be that hard. You got people running back and forth with cocaine and whores and blue movies every day. You'll get there.

He kisses my hand.

"Helped by Hick, once more," Parker says. "Good advice. Your advice was good last time too."

"Go," I say. I hand Thurman my navy-blue sports jacket. "It's not your size but it's not torn."

Thurman tries it on and it billows out behind him but it's respectable. I put my hand out for Thurman's and he kisses me on the cheek. He smells like honey. I hand Parker a black turtleneck.

"I don't have a necktie for you," I say, and I am almost crying.

"This is better than what I'm wearing. They'll think I'm bohemian," he says.

"Won't they just."

"I hope our paths cross again," Thurman says.

"In Cuernavaca," I say.

"In Cuernavaca."

He bows to Eleanor. Parker does the same and they're gone. Eleanor and I pick up the teacups and Parker's tumbler of Scotch and the bloody towels. She soaks the towels in the bathtub, with the last of our lemons, and I pack my things.

It's just brightening when I go down to the street. I put my hand up for a cab and one drives right up. I open the door and close it.

"Sorry," I say. "I forgot something."

I ring the doorbell and Eleanor opens it, expecting Tommie.

"I'm back."

She's still in her robe. She takes my hand, which is enough to make me cry, and she brings me into the bedroom, as if this is our dear and private place, where we must be, and that does make me cry. She's already made the bed. Her hat is on top of her closed suitcase. She sits down next to the suitcase and I sit in the old armchair.

"I packed last night," she says. "I couldn't sleep."

"Here's what I think," I say.

Eleanor says, "Do you want some tea? I can make tea."

"Here's what I think," I say. "You have such a big life ahead of you. I know you think it'll be mostly family, down to the great-grands and some ribbon-cutting and maybe there'll be some public school spelling bees, if you want to go out on a limb. Maybe you'll do some teaching, again."

"That doesn't sound too bad," she says.

She looks out the window.

"What a beautiful day," she says.

"Listen. I told you, you could write, and you wrote. Magazines, newspapers, books. You're Babe Ruth. You're a bestselling author, for Christ's sake. I told you you could turn the world upside down with those press conferences and you hit those out of the park. And I am telling you, people are going to turn to you. Everywhere. You're Franklin's legacy and one better and don't think Harry Truman doesn't know it. The man has his eye on you."

She sits back down on the bed.

"The story's over," she says.

I sit down beside her. "I heard. I heard you gave that line to the reporter. Humble. Very touching."

She smiles.

"You might be right," she says. "I might do a few good things, in the time I have left."

I sit next to her on the bed, so that we can both look out the window at the opening green and red buds.

"Damn right," I say. "And I'll be at home on Long Island, cheering like crazy, clipping your articles, waving to your plane overhead."

She pulls at the chenille dots on the bedspread.

"I'll need a press secretary, if I am doing all these grand things."

"You have Tommie for secretary and you have all those junior Tommies, the Tommie-ettes. And one of those girls will be articulate, silk-covered steel and she can do what you need done. That's not me."

"Not really silky," she says.

"Not really."

"You could handle the itineraries," she says. "Or you could just come. We'd have a wonderful time."

"You'll love it."

"You could love it," she says.

I kiss her hand.

"Lie down with me," I say.

"Tommie's coming," she says.

"She's not coming before eight."

Eleanor picks up her hat and moves it to the chair. I put the suitcase on the floor. I take off my coat. We don't take off anything else. We lie face-to-face on the bed, the ends of my red scarf lying on her kimono sleeve.

"What will you be doing?" she says.

"I told you, cheering you on. And walking the dog. I'll be writing. Planting peonies. Someone's gotta sit on that porch, Dearest."

"You'll love it," she says.

She sighs and I pat her face. I sigh too.

"What a pair we are," she says.

"That's the way to look at it. Not together, necessarily, but a pair, nonetheless."

"You're so cheerful," Eleanor says, and I am as angry with her as I have ever been.

She puts her hand on my shoulder. I rest my cheek against her hand. The sun is much higher now, and brightly yellow, in the clear blue sky.

We lie on the bed a few seconds more, forehead to forehead.

I say, Tommie will be here before you know it. I know, she says. I say that I'll write in a few days and Eleanor says, Do. She says, Of course I will too and we'll see each other, soonest.

Lilac and Star and Bird

· ·

SUNDAY, NOVEMBER 11, 1962
The Rectory Apartments
Hyde Park, New York

I dream about Eleanor's death.

I dream I'm in the Washington Square apartment, in the narrow kitchen, making tea and toast for us. The kitchen table is piled with dirty plates and cups, on top of the books I've written. I walk into the bedroom, with a tray, and Eleanor's lying on the bed in her pink nightgown, mouth open, eyes closed. I'm afraid to touch her but I can see she's dead. I get dressed in a hurry, wanting to leave before I'm discovered there but I hear sirens and I know they're coming for me. A broken window shade rattles in the dream and I wake up.

I dream Eleanor is at Val-Kill, walking alone through the autumn woods. She trips on a root and falls in slow motion, her cardigan rising like a sail behind her, her arms flying up, like a ballet dancer, and she hits her head on a rock. She lies there, faceup in the wet leaves, eyes open, bleeding out. The sun rises. I don't appear in this dream at all.

I dream I'm at the beach with Eleanor. We're in the wool bathrobes we wore at Campobello and we walk barefoot to the edge of the ocean. It's early. The sun is just rising through the clouds. We drop our robes and we are naked. We are girls in our twenties, as we never knew each other. The air is lush and light on our perfect bodies. We hold hands and walk into the sparkling water, slowly and quietly, as if it's sacred. We walk until the water closes over our heads, like a silk sheet. There's nothing frightening about it. I put my arms up and push the water aside. I'm not at all worried as I walk out, onto the sand. I walk to Eleanor's robe, lying in a heap, and I sit down next to it, crying in a girlish, theatrical way. Even in the dream, I'm disappointed in what a crybaby I am. Eleanor rises from the water and walks out. She shakes the sand out of her robe and pulls me up, close to her, before she puts it on. We are wet body to wet body, our heads on each other's shoulders. She kisses me and she is all brine and beach roses. She says, I died, you silly.

Eleanor and I had our last picnic, three months ago. It was August, still and sticky. We sat under the big maple tree in my yard. She'd made a grand tour, dedicating the FDR Bridge between Maine and Canada, seeing old friends all over the place and working for world peace, when she wasn't in bed, sick as a dog.

"Those transfusions for the anemia are terrible," she said. "I was running such a high fever, a month ago, I thought to myself, I could just give up and die."

"Please, don't," I said. "You've worn yourself out."

"I'm not afraid of dying. And I'm seventy-eight," Eleanor said. "I am allowed to be a little bit worn-out."

I laughed. I said that she'd worn out everyone around her years ago.

Eleanor lay down on the grass, carefully, and she put her head in my lap.

"Oh, this is what I needed," she said. "I might never get up."

"'Everyone has the right to rest and leisure, including reasonable limitation of working hours and periodic holidays with pay.' Article Twenty-four," I said. "It's a human right. You said so."

"You studied it," she said. "That declaration was what I was put on earth to do, and now I've done it."

"Close your eyes," I said. "I'm not going anywhere."

I thought that if we both died, right then, under the enormous green hands of the maple leaves, we would be delighted. We would start believing in God, I thought, just as we died. I held my breath for a few seconds, to encourage a heart attack.

"Listen," she said, poking me. "You're the only one who will listen to me. Do not let them keep me alive, just because they can. I don't want a thousand tests and a thousand treatments. I don't care if it's anemia or the common cold. I don't want David to show the world what a great doctor he is by throwing himself between me and death."

I don't find David Gurewitsch to be a great doctor. I'm not sure he's even a good doctor. He's got the accent and the manners and from where I stand now—very far from the Manhattan townhouse Eleanor's sharing with him and his wife, the malleable, wide-eyed Edna—the man has played my beloved like a violin. People talk, as they always do, but it's not much. Eleanor's an old lady now. David (Do call me David, he said. Don't bother with the title.) had the good sense to marry Edna, who's now making a career out of being Eleanor's little friend. The worst anyone can say is that Eleanor is generous with her friends and loves the company of clever, younger men. She says it herself. If she were a man, other old men would be slapping her on the back.

We talked for hours. I told her my book on American labor was coming along and that my book about Helen Keller was just made a Book-of-the-Month Club selection and she pulled me down and kissed me on the cheek.

"Tell me I was right," she said. "You're making money hand over fist, as they say, and young people love these books. Five books, Dearest. You are a proper and successful writer again. You have me to thank."

I stroked her forehead. "You were right. I have you to thank."

She struggled to sit up and we helped each other, like falling skaters, grabbing the lowest branches of the tree, clinging to the trunk, trying not to step on the dog. We were panting and laughing up to the house. I poured us a little Dubonnet so we could catch our breath.

"Look at this," she said, waving her hand down toward the tree. "I love this apartment. It's perfect for you."

"I like it," I said. "I miss my Little House but . . ."

"It's not Val-Kill," she said. "But even Val-Kill's not what it was. It's a madhouse. Did I tell you, Elliott sold Top Cottage."

"You told me." Elliott Roosevelt sold Hyde Park and the Roosevelt name and every Roosevelt thing he could get his hands on. He hustled soap and hairbrushes on his radio show, saying, It's the kind Mother uses. I would bring up Lucy Mercer before I would bring up those commercials.

"I'm sorry, Dearest," she said. "I shouldn't have let you go."

"Likewise," I said. "How do you like the place in New York, with David and Edna?"

She shrugged. "Very nice. I know what you think. You think he's a charming rogue—"

"Those baby blues," I said. "And so big on the hand-kissing."

"—and that once more I've been taken in by a man who needs a mother, and on top of that, I've adopted the wife, the baby, half a house, and the whole kit and caboodle."

"Well," I said. "Everyone needs a hobby."

She laughed and sipped her drink. I traced the veins on the back of her hand. She slipped her fingers through mine and I said, Our hands look like something from the Museum of Natural History.

"Dinosaurs," she said. "Do you remember our honeymoon to Vermont? You reciting Emily Dickinson, *ad alta voce*? Rowing in Eden. Perhaps all poetry should be shouted from a roadster—"

"By women madly in love," I said.

"Exactly."

"Wasn't that a time."

She held both my hands.

"Do not make me cry," she said. "Do not come visit me. You will have to run the Roosevelt gauntlet and you will hate what you see. And I will hate for you to see it. I am going to think of us, under this tree. Under this tree in your yard and under that beautiful tree in Maryland. Those cherry blossoms all over us? That's what I'll be thinking of."

We sat and held each other, twisting close in the kitchen chairs, until her car and driver appeared.

In October, she was in and out of the hospital. The newspapers got a tip, and no matter that she was First Lady to the World, no matter that she'd held a thousand press conferences and fought for freedom of the press everywhere she went, they all ran the same awful photo of her being carried out on a stretcher. She looked disheveled and disoriented and if you didn't know who you were looking at, you'd think victim of some natural disaster or plague because sick and old is essentially both of those things.

NOVEMBER 8 1962
THE FAMILY OF MRS FRANKLIN D ROOSEVELT INVITE YOU
TO THE CHURCH SERVICE TO BE HELD AT ST JAMES
EPISCOPAL CHURCH HYDE PARK NY SATURDAY NOVEMBER
10TH AT 2:00 PM AND TO THE INTERMENT SERVICE IN THE
ROSE GARDEN FRANKLIN D ROOSEVELT LIBRARY HYDE PARK
IMMEDIATELY FOLLOWING—PLEASE PRESENT THIS
TELEGRAM FOR ADMISSION

The new secretary was good enough to call me early in the morning. Maureen said Eleanor told her I had to be called before the telegram arrived. And so she was calling. I asked if they had let her die at home and she said yes. I asked who was with her, and she said, only the family, and I said, I was glad to hear it. She said to me, Mrs. R. wanted a plain pine box and she didn't want a public announcement to be made, until after the funeral. Fat chance, I said.

Crying in public upsets people, Eleanor used to say. Her grandmother always told her to cry in the bathroom. Her grandmother said, If you have to cry, go to the bathroom and run the taps. If I went to Eleanor's funeral, I'd be rending my garments and climbing into the grave. Eleanor would be horrified.

When Mary Todd Lincoln died, they flew the flag at half-staff, and I don't think this country has mourned a First Lady since. There'll be a trifecta of funerals, Hyde Park, Washington, and Manhattan, but Hyde Park is where the big shots will be. Truman, always a decent man, and Eisenhower, always a genial monster, and the ambassadors, the heads of state, governors, and some portion of the Supreme Court. Adlai Stevenson will be there. No one could keep him away, he loved her so. Marian Anderson will come and class the place up. All the Roosevelts, all twenty-seven grandchildren, plus spouses, the thirteen great-grandchildren, and every last Oyster Bay cousin, every single wife and stepchild. Every half brother and hanger-on, every illegitimate sprout and right behind them, with more teeth and more dimples, the persistent Kennedys (I was wrong about him, Eleanor said. His inaugural address was magnificent.) and Jackie, who has more up her pretty, couture sleeve than anyone think. Lyndon Johnson and Lady Bird, who knows how things should be done. What's left of the old crowd. The remaining Sapphic Sisters were there, I'm sure, and Joe and Trude, taking notes for his next book while they mourned, and the Gurewitsches, yielding softly to their elegant, telegenic grief.

I couldn't act as Eleanor would have liked, so I didn't go.

I am the last of our little tribe. I am the only one left who knows what *Abyssinia* means. I am the only person in the world who knows that when she said, *Je t'aime, je t'adore,* it wasn't just I love you, I adore you, in her fancy French, it was a promise to leave everything else behind, even if it was only for the length of the whispered call, for the three minutes stolen from the state dinner.

I don't know that she would feel this way, if she were the last of us.

I stayed in bed most of yesterday. It rained on and off. I walked the dog. Breakfast was the way it's become. Bran flakes more or less in the bowl, hot water on top of that because the milk had gone bad. My sense of smell is first-rate, still, and so is my hearing. If it takes me ten minutes to get out of bed, it takes closer to twenty and a few extra to find my slippers and not fall over while

I'm putting them on. I can still see shapes and colors and big signs and I can smell everything: the dog, last night's beef stew dinner, coffee, bananas, beer, pine trees, that terrible perfume Eleanor used to give to every luckless soul she met. Five small green bottles are still in my closet, in a shoe box. It's been seventeen years and I can still smell her own scent, salt and cucumber.

Under our breasts and in the creases, we smelled like fresh-baked bread in the mornings. We slept naked as babies, breasts and bellies rolling toward each other, our legs entwined like climbing roses. We used to say, we're no beauties, because it was impossible to tell the truth. In bed, we were beauties. We were goddesses. We were the little girls we'd never been: loved, saucy, delighted, and delightful.

We slept under a damp, clean, patched sheet with wind howling through the splits in the log cabin walls and I made tea from a kettle hung over the hearth. We hadn't been out of bed for hours. Eleanor sat up and said, We really should take a walk, and I said, Should we? Should we, really? I loved to see the quick dark flash of amusement in her eyes but this was nothing like that. Her eyes filled with tears.

"I do keep busy, darling. I have to. I would be undone with sadness, most of the time, otherwise. But not when I'm with you, not here."

Not now, I said. And we drank more tea, in front of the fire.

I can still see faces. I can see the general outline of things and some detail and most mornings, my left eye is pretty good and where that would have crushed me ten years ago, these days, a working left eye seems to be enough. I've done two more books, one-eyed, and I expect to do two more. Some mornings I contemplate Tolstoy's epilepsy and Byron's clubfoot and Milton's blindness, just to get myself going. Emily Dickinson said—or someone said that Emily Dickinson said—Rigor is no substitute for happiness. Nothing takes the place of happiness but I think rigor comes close. It's a comfort and a bulwark. The work rewards my attention. The sentences I wrote yesterday reassure me (when they don't appall me). I've had the same daily routine since Franklin died, and I love my schedule, like I love my dog, like I loved my cottage, like I love my apartment and my maple tree. Discipline, of all things, is now at the center of my life and I listen to the radio day and night, on a schedule. Morning is walk the dog and breakfast and the news. Lunch is half a sandwich and light entertainment and the O'Leary boy bringing me the mail and baseball news. Afternoon is me and the typewriter. Nighttime is dinner and the opera. Two hours on Sunday afternoon are reserved for tidying up and making a brisket and occasionally, visiting with my upstairs neighbor. We've discussed what I'm to do, if I find her body, and what she's to do, if she finds mine.

I can read for an hour or so at a time but I miss reading books by the boatload. I have stored up pages of poetry (O powerful western fallen star! O shades of night—O moody, tearful night) and I recite the lines while I cook, or walk the dog. Sometimes I do Sunny Florent's ballyhoo for the dog. I see Gerry's little white breast and feel its warm weight in my hand. I see women's bare bottoms, beckoning. I see Eleanor in every position, including a headstand, once, when I doubted her. I see my sister Myrtle's cold, cross little face when my father delivered me to the farm to cook and I wonder if that cold look was despair, not irritation, and I am sorry I didn't look for her, when I could have. I see Ruby from not so long ago and I'm sorry I haven't kept her closer. I see the several hats I stole, from several people, and I know I must have had my reasons. I see Eleanor, in a blue kimono, eating Chinese food on the bed in Washington Square. Grains of white rice are scattered all over the dark-blue silk. They've fallen so they look like snow on the embroidered bridge and willow trees. Eleanor wets her fingertip and picks them up, one by one.

I lean hard on my cane and the steps from my kitchen to the porch just about kill me tonight, but I fix my face, as Gerry used to say. The Reverend Gordon Kidd knocks on my door. He calls out, "How are you managing, Miss Hickok?" and I say, "Oh, better than some," and he chuckles and I pull myself together to walk to the car and make our raid on the Hyde Park cemetery. I don't know why this good man has offered to drive me to Eleanor's graveside but I think I can find the right moment to ask. My hope is that he'll say, I know what love looks like.

He takes my arm and he says, This is my privilege, Miss Hickok, and I say that I'm sorry that I've steered clear of his church. He laughs. He opens the car door and I heave myself in with the enormous jug of wildflowers I've put together, the kind you love, and there's not a carnation or chrysanthemum among them. But I'm wearing clothes that would distress you and I have no small talk for this nice man, who said such good and lovely things over your grave. (I heard on the radio. He said the world had suffered an irreparable loss, which is so true, and he said that the entire world would become one family as we are orphaned by your passing, which is probably not true.)

He drives me right past the big house, which has a lamp lit in one window, and he parks not too far from the rose garden. I can see the big white marble slab, marking your place and Franklin's. It's as bright as the moon. He says that he'll wait in the car for me, and I think he is so much your kind of person. He has probably noticed that I am half-blind and he has certainly noticed that I walk with a cane but he does nothing except hold the car door wide open for me.

I take small, slow steps, the way we have both come to these days, and it doesn't save me. My cane slides through wet leaves and I fall, onto my knees, which surprises me and it's so painful I cry out. The glass jug breaks on a rock. I put my hand over my mouth. Gordon Kidd comes by my side and helps me up. Be careful of the glass, he says. Please help me pick up the flowers, I say, and he does. I am a danger to myself in the dark. I don't want to make this nice man responsible for my little journey.

"There's a bench here, right around here," I say, and he helps me up. "Mrs. Roosevelt and I used to sit right around here."

We find the bench, which is cold, wet granite. I make a point of not complaining about my left knee, now pulsing so badly I feel the pounding from my hip to my hands.

"You go," I say. "You take the flowers and please lay them at the foot of her side of the grave. If you don't mind."

"I should take the flowers?"

"Please take them, and if you don't mind, just go back to the car."

I know what a believer you are in doing the thing well and I am sorry that I can't. The wildflowers are nothing to me now. I sit on our bench and talk to you. I am so sorry I couldn't go with you, on your big trip around the big world, and be who you needed me to be. I'm even more sorry that I didn't want to and that my plan for us seemed just as good to me as yours seemed to you. And now, all of those ups and downs, our separations and closed doors, those terrible fights and furies, our cruelties and our silences, seem like nothing, like losing a handbag or missing the morning train.

Reverend Kidd must have left the flowers with you already, because he passes by and says I should take my time.

. . .

The first thing I knew in this world was that I was alone and un-seen. Then I knew I was not. You are not just my port in the storm, which is what middle-aged women are supposed to be looking for. You are the dark and sparkling sea and the salt, drying tight on my skin, under a bright, bleaching sun. You are the school of minnows we walk through. You are the small fishing boat, the prow so faded you can hardly tell it's blue. You are the violet skies, rain spattering the sand until it's almost mud, and you are the light to come. You are the small, stucco houses with blue and white and flashing tin roofs, near the piers, and the dusty chickens that run through the café. You are the patched sail, and the hope-ful mast, and the frayed greenish ropes. You are the shells, the thin, pearly ones that almost crumble in your pocket and the wide blue ones that are like rough knives. You are the little girls, carry-ing water in their red buckets, and you are the ruined sandcastles at sunset, gaudy with seaweed and gull feathers. You are the dawn, rolling back the dark until the beach glitters and the girls return with their buckets, holding hands.

Author's Note

. . . .

To the best of my ability, I have worked from the particulars and facts of geography, chronology, customs, and books by actual historians. That said, this is a work of fiction, from beginning to end.

Acknowledgments

· ·

To say that I am lucky in my editor, Kate Medina, is like saying that I am lucky to be alive. I sure am, and you don't know the half of it.

My rare, unstoppable, and very dear agent, Jennifer Rudolph Walsh, has helped me and my books at every turn, with excellent judgment, unflinching candor, and reliable, unstinting kindness.

I've had the opportunity to work on this book, at length, at the MacDowell Colony, which is as close to writers' heaven as I ever need to be. I've continued to be a lucky visitor to the kitchen table of Jack O'Brien's Imaginary Farms, where I often get my best ideas, and to the Provincetown desk of Michael Cunningham, where I have been able to write them down, tear them up, and try again.

Wesleyan University, my alma mater and employer, has a wonderful library and wonderful librarians. It is a welcoming place for readers and writers, for teachers and students, and I am happier to be there than I ever imagined. The days spent at the FDR Presidential Library and Museum, and in their Archives, were among the most exciting and productive of my writing life.

I want to acknowledge, praise, and bow down to Blanche Wiesen Cook, whose exceptional biography of Eleanor Roosevelt inspired this book, as the author's commitment to truth, detail, and curiosity inspired me.

Three great writers, Bob Bledsoe, Tayari Jones, and Sarah Moon, read, criticized, consoled, and put out fires, right up until the last minute.

My children, Alexander, Caitlin, and Sarah, are my best and most demanding audience and my daily joy, enabling me to finish this book and keep sight of the rest of my life.

As she has for the last decade, my friend and assistant, Jennifer Ferri, talked me off a few ledges, stopped a few bullets with her golden bracelets, and, in every way, made my work possible.

I can never thank my husband, Brian, enough, although I try. He is my reader, my listener, and my deliverance.

Amy Bloom

....

WHITE HOUSES

A Reader's Guide

QUESTIONS AND TOPICS FOR DISCUSSION

. . . .

1. *White Houses* is a novel based on relationships and events that happened from the 1930s to the '60s. Did any historical information in the book interest or surprise you? Did you know anything about the Lindbergh baby kidnapping, the affair between Eleanor Roosevelt and Lorena Hickok, or FDR's affairs before reading the book?

2. Lorena had a very difficult childhood, filled with poverty, violence, and uncertainty. Eleanor also struggled with violence and uncertainty, but, because she was a Roosevelt, had every opportunity and comfort. How do you think their backgrounds affected who they became as adults, in both their personal and professional lives? Did it affect the dynamics of their relationship?

3. Lorena's short time in the circus introduced us to many unforgettable and unique characters on the outskirts of society. Who do you think Lorena most related to? Did you relate to any of them?

4. Lorena and Eleanor shared a love that was taboo because of how people viewed sexuality at the time and Eleanor's high-profile marriage. How do you think their love story would play out today? Do you think it would have ended differently, or the same?

5. Lorena and FDR had a complicated relationship—he was her president and her friend, and also her lover's husband. How did this affect Lorena's relationship with FDR, and her relationship with Eleanor?

6. *White Houses* is told from the perspective of Lorena, a woman on the sidelines of history who was literally cropped out of photos. How do you think her view of history differs from how other people viewed it? How do you think Eleanor and Lorena's story would have changed if it was told from the perspective of Eleanor, or FDR, or anyone else who worked at the White House?

7. Eleanor Roosevelt was a groundbreaking first lady, a politician and activist in her own right who even publicly disagreed with her husband's politics from time to time. Were you familiar with Eleanor Roosevelt's work before reading this novel? Were you surprised by her politics and behavior given the period she lived in? What could women today learn from her approach to politics?

8. Before covering the White House, Lorena established herself as a respected journalist, but was forced to give up her career for her relationship with Eleanor. What would you give up to be with the person you loved? Would you do what Lorena did? What have you given up for love?

PHOTO: © ELENA SEIBERT

AMY BLOOM is the author of *Come to Me,* a National Book Award finalist; *A Blind Man Can See How Much I Love You,* nominated for the National Book Critics Circle Award; *Love Invents Us; Normal; Away,* a *New York Times* bestseller; *Where the God of Love Hangs Out;* and *Lucky Us,* a *New York Times* bestseller. Her stories have appeared in *The Best American Short Stories, O. Henry Prize Short Stories, The Scribner Anthology of Contemporary Short Fiction,* and many other anthologies here and abroad. She has written for *The New Yorker, The New York Times Magazine, The Atlantic Monthly, Vogue, O: The Oprah Magazine, Slate, Tin House,* and *Salon,* among other publications, and has won a National Magazine Award. She is the Shapiro-Silverberg Professor of Creative Writing at Wesleyan University.

amybloom.com
Facebook.com/AmyBloomBooks
Twitter: @AmyBloomBooks

Chat.
Comment.
Connect.

Visit our online book club community at
Facebook.com/RHReadersCircle

Chat
Meet fellow book lovers and discuss what you're reading.

Comment
Post reviews of books, ask—and answer—thought-provoking
questions, or give and receive book club ideas.

Connect
Find an author on tour, visit our author blog, or invite one of
our 150 available authors to chat with your group on the phone.

Explore
Also visit our site for discussion questions, excerpts, author
interviews, videos, free books, news on the latest releases,
and more.

Books are better with buddies.
Facebook.com/RHReadersCircle

RANDOM HOUSE READER'S CIRCLE ®

RANDOM HOUSE